THE MYSTERY OF THE FACTITIOUS FALCONER

THE THREE INVESTIGATORS

IN

THE MYSTERY OF THE
FACTITIOUS
FALCONER

BY

ELIZABETH ARTHUR
& STEVEN BAUER

BASED ON CHARACTERS
CREATED BY ROBERT ARTHUR

Hollow Tree Press 2025

CONTENTS

1

A Peculiar Encounter

"En garde," said Jupiter Jones.

He lunged forward, the tip of his sword pointed at the white chest of the masked man opposite him. His opponent stepped backwards and deftly parried Jupiter's thrust, sweeping the blade of his foil aside. Then he seized the momentum and rushed at Jupiter, forcing him back. Their blades clicked and clashed several times in rapid succession before the man feinted, and, in the opening the feint created, touched the tip of his foil to Jupiter's chest.

"Touché!" he cried.

He lowered his foil, reached up, grabbed the chin of his wire-mesh mask, and swept it off.

"That was an excellent first lesson, Jupiter," Mr. Rasmussen said. "You show real promise. You learn quickly, your reflexes are sharp, and you're quick on your feet."

Jupiter took off his own mask and smiled in thanks. He was at the Center for Falconry and Fencing – about twenty minutes from Rocky Beach. It would be his fourteenth birthday soon, and his Aunt Mathilda and his Uncle Titus had given him three fencing lessons as a present.

"I'm starting at Rocky Beach High in a few weeks," Jupiter said to Mr. Rasmussen, "and everybody picks a sport to focus on. I'm thinking of choosing fencing, but the fencing club has only four members, and I'd hate to feel I'd let anyone down if I joined and then dropped out."

"There may be only four fencers at Rocky Beach High," Mr. Rasmussen said, "but there are twenty fencing clubs here in southern California alone. Our sport doesn't grab headlines, but it's alive and well. It's a sport where it doesn't matter how big or strong you are; what matters is how you respond to the other fencer."

Jupiter unbuttoned the snaps on his fencing jacket; it was warm in the gym.

"That's what I think I'm going to like about it," said Jupiter. "Thank you for the lesson. I'll see you again in a few days."

In the locker room, Jupiter showered and changed back into his street clothes, then took the fencing outfit, mask, and foil to the equipment room. The lesson had indeed been enjoyable, and Jupiter was beginning to think that maybe fencing *was* the sport for him. It focused the mind; it required extreme concentration, heightened awareness, and split-second reflexes. And while it could be instinctive and lightning-fast in terms of its moves, there was something cerebral about it that appealed to him.

Jupiter left the equipment room and walked back through a maze of hallways toward the reception area where William Worthington was waiting for him. Years before, when Jupiter had won a contest whose prize was the use of a gold-plated vintage Rolls-Royce, complete with chauffeur, Worthington had been the chauffeur. He'd become a friend and advisor to The Three Investigators detective firm Jupiter had founded with his best friends Pete Crenshaw and Bob Andrews, and when Jupiter's aunt and uncle had told Worthington that they wanted to do something special for his birthday this year, Worthington had suggested lessons at the Center for Falconry and Fencing.

Worthington himself had learned to fence there when he'd first come to southern California from England with hopes of a movie career, and after he, Bob, Pete, and Jupiter had seen live fencing in a recent production of a Shakespeare play, Worthington had encouraged Jupiter to try the sport.

His part of the birthday present was driving Jupiter to and from the lessons, and Jupiter was grateful to him for suggesting the idea to Aunt Mathilda and Uncle Titus. Unexpectedly, he was also grateful that there had been a break in The Three Investigators' hectic schedule. It had given him time to get caught up on some reading, and also to research fencing in advance of this first lesson.

Now the school year was right around the corner, and although Jupiter was feeling proud that he, Pete, and Bob had managed to solve five quite different – and quite complex – mysteries since school had let out in June, he was also wondering if something else would come their way in the next two weeks. The cases they'd solved so far had taken them to California's gold country; to Sonoma, north of San Francisco; to Jackson, where Jupiter had discovered some previously unknown relatives of his mother; and most recently up the southern coast to Isla Vista and a wild boat chase across the Pacific to Santa Catalina Island.

Between hidden treasure, forged documents, counterfeiters, nefarious schemes at a theater, and the illegal animal trade, it had been an eventful summer, Jupiter thought.

And it wasn't over yet. In a few days, he, Pete, and Bob – together with their new friend Mallory MacLeod – would be going to a party at the home of John Lysander Smith and his partner Cornelius Patterson. The Three Investigators had met Lyle – as he liked to be called – when they were in search of a missing quilt of historic significance, but the party was a fund-raiser of sorts. While Jupiter was a bit unclear what the funds were being raised for, he knew it had something to do with art, because Lyle had had a long career as a museum curator, and Cornelius was an art restorer.

Jupiter wasn't particularly looking forward to the party – in general he disliked formal, fancy parties, which he found loud, jangly, and filled with superficial conversation – but Lyle had invited Mallory and The Three Investigators because an art dealer friend had a fourteen-year-old German nephew visiting for the summer, and Lyle had thought the nephew might enjoy meeting The Three Investigators – who he seemed to have heard of, somehow. Bob had accepted the invitation on behalf of all of them, Jupiter thought ruefully.

When he finally got to the grand Spanish mission-style lobby of the Center for Falconry and Fencing, Jupiter found Worthington studying a large oil painting. Jupiter had noticed it on his way in, but he hadn't really looked at it, and as he went to stand beside Worthington, he found the painting rather striking.

In it, a man stared boldly at the viewer. He was wearing what looked to Jupiter like medieval clothing – a bright green fur-trimmed belted tunic that hung down below his waist, tight-fitting black trousers, black boots, and a flat fur hat. His right elbow was raised and crooked, and his hand and forearm were sheathed by a dark leather glove and gauntlet.

On the gauntlet was perched an almost-pure-white falcon, calm and composed – his eyes staring at the viewer with the same unwavering concentration as the falconer.

"It's rather good, isn't it?" Worthington said. "Much more authoritative than I would have expected for a painting hanging in a lobby. I don't remember it from my own days in training at the Center."

"It *is* good," Jupiter said, nodding. He wasn't particularly knowledgeable about art, but several times, in past cases, The Three Investigators had encountered an art thief called Huganay, and Jupiter had had the opportunity to see some very fine paintings at very close range.

As well, the few times he'd been in an art museum − usually as part of a school field trip − he'd found himself struck by certain paintings he'd later come to discover were widely acknowledged to be great.

Of course, this painting wasn't that, but Jupiter agreed with Worthington that what they were looking at was far above the ordinary. An artist had painted it − not an amateur, but a true artist. It would have been hard to explain to anyone how he knew this, but he did. As he studied the painting, he noticed that there were two letters − the letters "T" and "A" − on the leather gauntlet. He wondered if it was a custom in falconry for the falconer to put his initials on his gauntlet.

"Did you enjoy the fencing?" Worthington asked, turning away and looking inquiringly at Jupiter.

"Very much," Jupiter told him. "At the beginning, I was thinking too hard, but by the end, I was acting more instinctively − trusting that I would know what to do next."

Worthington smiled.

"As I imagined," he said. "It's just like life that way. If you stick with it, I think you could do very well."

The entrance to the lobby featured a modern, pneumatic glass door, but there was a side door opening onto an interior Spanish-style courtyard, and as he glanced outside, Worthington caught sight of a man sitting on a stone bench under an olive tree.

"Good Lord!" he said. "That's my old fencing teacher! I had no idea he still worked here. Why don't you make an appointment for your next lesson while I go say hello to him?"

Jupiter nodded, so Worthington pushed open the door into the courtyard and strode through it.

"Otto!" he called, while Jupiter started toward the glass window behind which the receptionist sat.

Just at that moment, the pneumatic glass door swung open and a man came in.

He looked to Jupiter as if he were in his late 40s. He was very tall and slender. He wore pointy black leather shoes with dark purple laces, tight black pants, and a very closely cut violet shirt. His rust-colored hair was stylishly cropped and he wore a pair of rectangular glasses with black plastic frames that made his eyes look like side-by-side billboards.

Once the door had closed behind him with a whoosh, the man stopped and glanced around, as if he were looking to see how many people would look back at him. Although there were only two people in the lobby – Jupiter and the receptionist – Jupiter sensed that the new arrival liked being looked at, and was used to it. The man's eyes fell on the painting of the medieval falconer and lingered there for a moment, but when he saw Jupiter looking at him, he nodded his head briskly – though somehow also condescendingly – then moved with a confident air toward the glass window behind which the receptionist sat.

Her name was on a card on the window. It read Joanna Schultz.

"Can I help you?" she asked.

The man smiled at her with what seemed to Jupiter a sort of pity.

"Vell, madame, I certainly hope so," he said. "I hope so very much. As you can tell from my accent, I am a German visitor to your country. At least, I assume it is your country – that you are part of the great American experiment. One of its mongrels, so to speak. Though your name, of course, is German."

The receptionist's face clouded slightly, and she said – very sensibly, in Jupiter's opinion – "America stopped being an experiment a long time ago. I'm an American citizen, if that's what you mean."

"Of course you are," the man replied. "My name is Günther Böhm." He paused, as if to give time for his name to sink in. "Although I live in the city of Berlin, I'm in California for a few months while my work is exhibited at an art gallery in Los Angeles. Yes," he added brightly, "I am indeed *that* Günther Böhm! Most truly, a citizen of the world!"

"Really?" Joanna Schultz said drily. She had clearly never heard of Günther Böhm but considered it rude to say so.

"Really," Günther Böhm said. "But today I've driven out to your delightfully quaint Center because I've always wanted to fly falcons. I love the idea of them dropping so suddenly and ruthlessly on their prey! My grandfather was a falconer, and I want to learn as much as I can in five or six weeks."

"Falcons are fast, but falconry isn't," said Joanna Schultz. "Most of our clients work with a raptor for a year or more."

Günther Böhm flashed an insincere smile. "I'm sure," he said, spreading his fingers wide and displaying his palms in a gesture that seemed to Jupiter like something he'd done again and again. "Unfortunate, my length of stay," he added. "But, of course, in a way, I feel I already *am* a falconer! My art is bold and far-sighted – very honest. It looks life in the eye! If it would help, I could pay double for lessons. Luckily for me, although my falconer grandfather was only a Wehrmacht officer, my father was a rich industrialist."

"Really?" Joanna Schultz said again – and this time with what seemed to Jupiter like obvious distaste. She handed Günther Böhm a rate sheet and said, "Our fees are fixed. Paying double won't be necessary."

"How kind of you to say that! So maybe a time or two? Just to get a sense of what it feels like to have a falcon on my wrist? And today, might I meet one of your teachers and get a tour of this building, and perhaps the mews?"

"I'll have to see," Joanna Schultz responded. "Please take a seat while I talk to Mr. Hutchinson."

As Ms. Schultz walked out of her office, Günther Böhm turned and saw Jupiter looking at him. Jupiter was still standing by the painting, and the self-described German visitor to America decided to join him there, rather than to sit down.

"What have we here?" he said as he strode across the room. He crossed his arms on his chest as if this engaged his critical faculties, and he made little humming noises as he studied the canvas. Then he turned his head to speak to Jupiter, who noticed that he smelled faintly of cigar smoke.

"There are things to admire," he said, "in even the most amateurish painting, don't you think, young man?"

"I don't think this painting is amateurish," Jupiter said. "I think it's very good."

Günther Böhm looked at him as though he found the remark amusing. "I just find realism very dull. Banal. Unsurprising. In my opinion, true art began with German expressionism. So broad, so strong, so emotional," he said.

Jupiter had no idea what German expressionism was, and didn't much want to at the moment.

He wished that Worthington would stop talking to his old fencing teacher and rejoin him, but he felt awkward about just walking away from this obnoxious man. After all, he really *was* a visitor to the country, and, like Joanna Schultz, Jupiter didn't want to seem as unfriendly as he felt. He searched his mind for a topic that would put an end to the discussion about art.

"You said your grandfather was an officer in the Wehrmacht?" Jupiter asked. "That was the German Army under Hitler, wasn't it?"

As was frequently the case, Jupiter had no idea why he knew this – he knew little about the Second World War – but after he had heard something once, even in passing, he almost always remembered it forever.

"Yes. Oh, yes," said Günther Böhm. "*He* was not an artist; he merely collected paintings. Pretty paintings, like this one. My father collected even more of them. And he was not really my grandfather, either. My so-called "father" was his son, but I was adopted, so I don't feel I've inherited the blood guilt of my Nazi ancestor. *I* am not responsible for my grandfather's crimes."

Though Günther Böhm laughed lightly and smiled brightly when he said this, it seemed to Jupiter a peculiar thing for him to say. Adopted or not, no one could reasonably be held responsible for the crimes of one of their grandfathers, he thought.

Luckily, just then, Joanna Schultz returned with a burly man in overalls who beckoned to Günther Böhm and told him he was ready to show him around the facility.

Böhm clicked his heels together and

bowed his head slightly. "Goodbye, my fellow art lover," he said to Jupiter, then strode away – leaving Jupiter feeling oddly unsettled.

However, with Worthington still talking to his old friend, at least Jupiter was now able to go up to the glass window and make an appointment for another fencing lesson in two days' time. While he was there, he asked Joanna Schultz if she knew where the painting of the falconer had come from.

Ms. Schultz told him that the Danish actor Per Jorgensen had been trained by the Center in both falconry and fencing for a movie set in the Middle Ages. After he'd been nominated for an Oscar for the role, he'd bought and donated the painting as a thank-you. Since the Center had only had it for a month or so, she explained, they hadn't yet put up a plaque with Per Jorgensen's name on it.

Jupiter thanked Ms. Schultz for the information, then decided to wait for Worthington outside. He pulled open the pneumatic door and walked into the bright California sunshine. Once there, he saw the ash-tipped stub of a very thin cigar, as well as a match book, on the ground. From the cigar smoke Jupiter had smelled on Günther Böhm, he presumed that Böhm must have been the litterer.

When he bent down to pick the litter up and deposit it in a nearby trash can, his presumption was confirmed by the fact that the matchbook had a sparkly purple cover that read *Berlin Bohemien Nachtclub*.

On a whim, Jupiter thrust the matchbook into a pocket and was just depositing the cigar stub in a trash bin when Worthington appeared from the lobby.

"I'm sorry," he said to Jupiter. "I didn't mean to keep you waiting as long as that. I hadn't seen Otto for years, and there was a lot to catch up on."

"I didn't mind at all," Jupiter said.

He didn't mention his encounter with Günther Böhm, but filled Worthington in on what Joanna Schultz had told him about the painting of the falconer as the two of them headed for the Ford Flex. The Three Investigators had bought the car earlier that summer with reward money they'd been given by a client – the retired history teacher Isabella Chang.

At some point in one of their meetings, she'd implied she was looking for a housemate, and in the course of their last case, The Three Investigators had introduced her to a retired English teacher – a man who'd fought in the

Second World War, Jupiter suddenly reflected – and the two of them were now sharing Isabella's house on the edge of Rocky Beach.

Worthington started the engine and headed toward home. "Did you ever go back to visit Isabella and Wally?" Jupiter asked. "I remember they invited you."

"I certainly did," said Worthington. "They served me tea and biscuits by the koi pond and asked me how you and Pete and Bob had met. I told them you'd met in kindergarten – though I don't think I mentioned that the three of you have been celebrating your birthdays together for almost nine years now!"

That was true, Jupiter thought. Since their birthdays all took place within six weeks of one another, the three boys had celebrated together from an early age. One year they had a party at Bob's, the next at Pete's, and the third at Jupiter's. This year it was Jupiter's turn. Jupiter's birthday came first, on August 18 – followed by Bob's on September 10, and Pete's on October 3.

"It's my turn to host the party this year," Jupiter said. "Or rather, it's Uncle Titus and Aunt Mathilda's turn. But I'm going to propose we hold it in the Rocky Beach City Park, since the guest list promises to be bigger than in the past. Pete and Bob and I are meeting to plan the party this afternoon."

"A fine way to end the summer," said Worthington. "Do you also have another case on tap?"

"Not yet," said Jupiter, "but since Pete and Bob and I don't think we should count on investigating cases during the school year, I'm hoping we'll have one last case before school starts."

Back at the Salvage Yard Jupiter thanked Worthington again – not just for driving him to the Center but also for suggesting the lessons to his aunt and uncle. The next lesson was the day after tomorrow, first thing in the morning, and Worthington promised to pick Jupiter up a half hour before the lesson started. Then he drove away.

Jupiter didn't expect Pete and Bob for a while yet, so he went to the office to check in with Aunt Mathilda. He was surprised to find his uncle there as well.

"It's my swashbuckling nephew!" Uncle Titus said. "Douglas Fairbanks and Errol Flynn, look out! What do you think, Mathilda? A career in the movies?"

Aunt Mathilda gave Uncle Titus a withering look. "That's not funny, Titus," she said.

"Jupiter is still trying to forgive me."

Jupiter smiled. When he had been very young, his aunt had pushed him to become a child actor, and it had turned out badly.

"Let's not talk about that again," Jupiter said. "I forgive you."

His aunt looked flabbergasted. "Really?" she said. "Land sakes!"

"Really," Jupiter said, and meant it. It had taken a long time, but he had finally forgiven her; he knew she had meant well.

"Will wonders never cease!" Uncle Titus said. "Now here's a puzzle for you, Jupiter."

Jupiter had recently tired of his uncle's puzzles, but at least this time he was not being asked to perform before an audience.

"I've been meaning to ask you, Uncle Titus – " he began.

"I know, I know," Uncle Titus said. "You're too old for this. But humor me just this once more." He paused. "I made this one up, especially for you," he said. "What is it that wounds a foe, encircles a town, and profits from another man's goods?" Uncle Titus asked.

Jupiter was used to logical puzzles from Uncle Titus, but this one was different. This was more like a classic riddle, though it seemed to lack the play on words that was so common to riddles. Aunt Mathilda was smiling at him expectantly. Like her husband, she had become very proud of her nephew's abilities. Wounds a foe, Jupiter thought. Encircles a town. And then, he realized he was thinking too hard.

"Fencing," he said.

Uncle Titus roared with appreciation. "That's my boy!" he said, clapping his hands. "I knew you wouldn't let me down."

"Congratulations, Uncle Titus," Jupiter said. "That was clever."

Uncle Titus smiled bashfully.

"Now don't go giving the old codger a big head," Aunt Mathilda said. "That's all I need. Would you do me a favor and go to Leif and Magnus's workshop? I want to know how that quarter-sawn oak dining table is coming along. The client is quite insistent."

Leif and Magnus Haldorsson were the Salvage Yard's resident carpenters – two Norwegian brothers in their twenties, who had started working for Jupiter's aunt and uncle late the previous spring. Both were tall and lean and blond and looked quite alike, though Magnus had been growing a beard, which had shades of red in it. Leif was the elder and had a sunny and carefree disposition, while

Magnus was his polar opposite – someone for whom every silver lining had a cloud.

Jupiter, Pete, and Bob had become quite fond of them; they were fine additions to the life of the Salvage Yard. They were also excellent workmen, as The Three Investigators had already known when – earlier that summer – Bob had had the idea to hire the two of them to make a reproduction immigrant's trunk as a thank-you present for Mallory MacLeod.

She and her mother had recently moved to Rocky Beach from Scotland, where Mallory had grown up, after her father had unexpectedly died, and she'd become friends with Bob, and then with Pete and Jupiter, and had been genuinely helpful with a number of their cases that summer.

In addition, Aunt Mathilda had hired Mallory to inventory some of the Salvage Yard's treasures for a new website that would be going online any time now, and Aunt Mathilda had recently told Jupiter that she didn't know how she had managed before Leif, Magnus, and Mallory had all arrived at the Salvage Yard.

However, of the three of them, it had been Mallory who had made the biggest difference in Jupiter's personal life. Before she had stopped by the Salvage Yard to examine a suit of armor by the gate, he had really never imagined that a girl with her startling — well, looks — could also be so intelligent and tenacious. She didn't seem to be here right at the moment, and Jupiter was surprised to find he was disappointed not to be able to tell her about his just-finished fencing lesson — and even his meeting with Günther Böhm.

"Well?" his aunt said meaningfully.

"I'll be happy to go to the Haldorsson's workshop," Jupiter said. "Though first I want to go back to the house and change my clothes."

"All right, but don't dawdle!" Aunt Mathilda told him, so Jupiter walked briskly through the gate at the back of the Salvage Yard that led to his aunt and uncle's house and ran up to his bedroom. Before he folded the pants he'd been wearing, he reached into his pocket to transfer his Swiss Army knife, his billfold containing a stash of Three Investigators cards, and various other items he kept with him at all times.

While he was doing this, his fingers closed on the matchbook with the sparkly purple cover that Günther Böhm had dropped on the ground outside the Center for Falconry and

Fencing – the matchbook from the *Berlin Bohemien Nachtclub*. Idly, Jupiter opened it and was surprised to find what looked like a telephone number written in purple ink on the inside top cover. The number began with +49 and ran on in an unfamiliar arrangement of numbers and spaces.

Since Jupiter had long been accustomed to analyzing both his feelings and his thoughts, it didn't take him long to realize that the feeling he had as he looked at these numbers was the wish that they were a clue to something. They weren't, of course – they were simply a phone number hastily scrawled on a matchbook – but they made Jupiter realize that he really *did* want to solve one more case this summer, and before he left his bedroom to go visit Leif and Magnus's workshop, he carefully set the matchbook on the windowsill near his desk.

2

A Haldorsson Family Tale

As Jupiter was setting the match book on his window sill, Bob Andrews was biking toward the Salvage Yard with a pot of blue geraniums in his backpack. Bob's father had been given them by a woman he worked with at The Los Angeles *Sun*. Apparently she had a crush on him, because she'd told him the blue of the flowers matched the blue of his eyes. Yikes, as Pete would say!

Since Bob's father hadn't wanted to be rude, he'd taken the flowers home with him, then asked Bob whether he thought Mathilda Jones might like them. He knew she had a number of pots of flowers on the porch of her office at the Salvage Yard – including some geraniums.

Although Bob didn't know anything about flowers, to him it seemed as if Aunt Mathilda's red geraniums and the blue geraniums in his backpack were completely different kinds of plants. Even so, he was perfectly willing to pass the flowers on and had placed them into his backpack in such a way that they wouldn't get crushed during the journey.

Bob was glad to be back in Rocky Beach. He liked his hometown, and he hadn't gotten to spend much time in it this summer. Of the five cases The Three Investigators had solved, only one had kept them close to home. Otherwise they'd been all over the state of California.

However, things were settling down now. That morning, Bob's father had taken him shopping for school clothes and school supplies, and they'd had a great time together. Among the things they'd discussed was the last case The Three Investigators had been involved in – a case in the course of which Bob and Pete had been kidnapped on a sailboat by a couple of animal smugglers. Although Bob had been in similar kinds of danger at various times in the past, there'd been something about this time that had been different.

Maybe it was just that he was older than he'd been on previous occasions, or maybe it was the fact that the kidnapping had been at sea, but when one of the men had tied Bob's hands behind him and made threatening comments about Bob and Pete's probable fate, Bob had ended up thinking about how the history of humanity was filled with events in which one group of human beings hurt another group – and frequently got away with it, particularly in times of war.

That was really what it had felt like, for a while, when Bob and Pete had been sailing into the darkness somewhere in the Pacific Ocean – as if they had somehow found themselves captured in the middle of a war.

Although Bob's father earned his living as a journalist, not a historian, he and Bob shared a fascination with history that frequently led to the two of them watching documentaries together on the History Channel, or **PBS**, or **BBC** America. In fact, they had recently seen a documentary about a failed assassination attempt on the life of Adolf Hitler.

It had surprised Bob – though not his father – to learn that Hitler had been feared and hated not only by the countries he went to war with, but by many, many Germans, including many who were professional soldiers in the German Army. It had surprised them *both* to learn Adolf Hitler had wanted to be an artist when he was young, and at the age of eighteen had moved to the Austrian capital of Vienna to study art.

The documentary – *Operation Valkyrie* – had explained that although Hitler had applied for admission to the famous Vienna Academy of Fine Arts, he hadn't been accepted, because although he'd actually been a decent artist, his paintings hadn't been in the preferred style of the times. This morning, Bob and his father had talked about the fact that if Hitler had been allowed to study art as a young man, all the terrible things Germany had done in the Second World War might never have happened.

But then Bob's father had remarked that, even if Hitler *had* become an artist, someone else might have led Germany into a ruinous war. After all, he had said, there were always a lot of people who thought they could justify doing ghastly things to other people, or other people's countries.

As Bob arrived at the large filigreed wrought-iron gates that marked the front entrance to the Jones Salvage Yard, he spotted Jupiter coming through the gate at the back of the Yard, and all thoughts of the Second World War vanished. He climbed off his bicycle, leaned it against the office, unbuckled his helmet, and took the flowerpot out of his backpack.

He waved to Jupiter. "Jupe!" he said. "How did your fencing lesson go?"

"I liked it," Jupiter said. "My teacher explained that fencing is a sport in which it doesn't matter how big or strong you are. What matters is how you respond to the other fencer. That makes it a lot like being an investigator trying to outwit an adversary."

"Then it's a perfect sport for you, Jupe!" Bob exclaimed.

He'd barely had time to finish this sentence when the morning was shattered by Pete's arrival. Standing on the pedals of his bike, pumping hard as he turned the last corner, Pete careened through the entrance with a squeal of brakes and a spray of gravel. When he saw Bob and Jupiter, he hooted and waved, then jumped off his bike, shoved it next to Bob's, and started talking.

"I can't believe another year has passed!" he said. "And I had a great idea! How about if we invite Rafael and Elena to our birthday party?"

Rafael was a Chumash Indian – well, half Chumash and half Hispanic – who the boys had met on their last case. Rafael had driven the boat that had rescued Bob and Pete after they'd been kidnapped.

"That *is* a great idea," Bob said. "I think we should also invite Isabella Chang and Wally

Tate."

"I see The Three Investigators are all on the same wavelength," Jupiter said. "Because I thought it would be good to invite my family from Jackson – and maybe Branko Petrovich, although I'm afraid he won't be able to come. Too close to the start of the school year."

Earlier that summer, The Three Investigators had met a Serbian boy who had invited them to come stay at his family's vineyard in Jackson, where Jupiter had discovered relatives of his mother he hadn't known he'd had. Bob thought it had been a very good thing for him.

"So, I was thinking," Jupiter went on. "We'd normally have the party at my house this year, but it's not a very big house. What do you think about having the party at the Rocky Beach City Park?"

"That's a great idea, too!" said Pete. "We could have a hundred people and they'd all fit in the park!"

"I don't think there will be a hundred," Jupiter said, "but we might have twenty-five or thirty, what with the Pelletiers, and Rafael and Elena, and Isabella and Wally – "

"Maybe we could also invite Califia Garcia-Williams," Pete said. "And Charlotte Mitchell."

"And Leif and Magnus," Bob said. "And Mallory, of course."

Jupiter and Pete looked at him as though he'd just stated the most obvious thing in the world.

"Of course!" they said, almost in unison.

"I have some other ideas, too," Jupiter added. "But they can wait until we get to Headquarters. Right now I have to ask Leif and Magnus something for my aunt. Why don't the two of come with me? By the way, Bob, why are you holding a flowerpot?"

Bob grimaced. "It's a present from my father to Aunt Mathilda," he said. "A woman at work gave it to him, but he didn't want it. I'll give it to her later. I'll say hello to Leif and Magnus first."

Ever since the Norwegian carpenters had finished the immigrant's trunk The Three Investigators had commissioned, Bob had liked visiting the brothers to see what they were doing. As he followed Jupiter through the open door to their workshop, he was surprised to see three heads, not two, turn in his direction.

The third face he'd never seen before, but it looked so much like the others that he knew before being told that this had to be Leif and Magnus's sister.

Her face was slender and her eyes blue; though she used no makeup, her cheekbones were highly colored. Bob thought she was very pretty. Her long fine hair was white-blond, gathered into a braid that hung over her left shoulder. In her tie-dyed blouse with its bursts of purple and yellow and red and a simple pair of jeans, she looked a bit like a modern-day hippie. She seemed to be about the same age as the three of them.

"Hello, Jupiter, Pete, and Bob!" Leif said. "Come meet our sister Freya. She already knows *you,* of course – or at least she knows Bob!"

He looked at Magnus and smiled broadly.

"Oh, yes," Magnus agreed, though his voice sounded characteristically gloomy. "She's become quite the expert on The Three Investigators."

Bob paused to take off his backpack and set it down near the doorway, along with the potted geranium. He wondered what Magnus could mean. Then he followed Jupiter over to where the other three were gathered.

"How do you do?" Bob said. There was an awkward silence as everyone looked at everyone else.

"Freya's about to start high school in Palisade Point," Leif explained. "Since it's where we all live with our parents."

"That's an unusual name," Bob said. It was the only thing he could think of to say.

"She was named after a Norse goddess who can change fate by weaving new elements into it," Leif responded.

Freya shrugged, as if to acknowledge that *she* had no special powers.

"Leif and Magnus and I were all given our names because of a friend of our grandfather's," she said. "When they were boys, he told Grandfather that if he ever had children he'd name them Leif, Magnus, Freya, and Frigg."

"If he ever had *four* children," Magnus said.

Freya laughed, rather disarmingly, Bob thought.

"Anyway," she said. "Grandfather's friend died young, and Grandfather had only one child – "

"Our father, Magnus, Sr.," said Leif.

"So *he* was the one who wound up doing the naming," Freya said. "Frigg never arrived, but the rest of us did."

"Though you came later than expected," Leif said to his sister. "We waited around for more than a decade. But you got here in time to play 'Odin's Hammer.'"

"What's that?" Bob asked.

"An online role-playing game," Magnus said. "Freya's been playing it all summer."

"I was thirteen when Freya was born," added Leif, "and Magnus was eleven. Freya was only six when our parents moved to California, but she still speaks fluent Norwegian – though she appreciates good English when she reads it!"

"Yes," Freya said. She flashed an annoyed look at Leif. "My brothers love to tease me. At home they've talked a lot about the Salvage Yard, and of course they mentioned The Three Investigators. So I looked you up online. I've seen your photographs."

So *that* was why she knew who the three of them were, Bob thought. It had been Pete's idea that Bob should put their photographs on the website where he was posting his reports of their adventures.

Freya was staring at Bob so intently that if he hadn't known they'd never met before, he might have thought they were old friends. He felt a bit thrown off balance.

"What Leif meant before about me appreciating good English," Freya said. "That was his way of saying how much I've enjoyed reading your case reports this summer."

"Really?" Bob said. Now *he* was embarrassed! Though he wanted people to like what he'd written, he'd found he was bad at accepting compliments.

"Yes," Freya said. "You have a real gift for creating characters."

Desperate to change the subject, Bob asked, "Is this the first time you've been to the Salvage Yard?"

"Yes," Freya said. "My parents thought I should get out of the house for a while. And my brothers are helping me make a loom."

"So you really *are* a weaver, then?" Bob said.

"Not really," said Freya. "But my grandfather sent me a bunch of skeins of hand-dyed wool before he died, and I've wanted to make something to remind me of him."

Up to this point in the conversation, Pete had been uncharacteristically silent, but now he asked, "When did he die?"

"Almost a year ago," Freya said.

"His name was Håkon Haldorsson," said Leif. "He was a great man. During the Second World War he worked with the Norwegian Resistance."

Bob knew from *Operation Valkyrie* that every country Hitler occupied had had a Resistance, and that in every country, it had been very dangerous work. Many men and women had been shot as traitors.

"That's really impressive," Bob said.

"What was the Norwegian Resistance?" asked Pete.

"After the Nazis occupied Norway," Magnus explained, "men like our grandfather joined together with others to do everything they could to sabotage the occupation forces. Grandfather used to tell me and Magnus stories about himself and his friend Bjørn Kalberg. Kalberg was the one who gave our grandfather the list of names. He was also a falconer; he had a gyrfalcon who came when he whistled. The stories Grandfather told about himself and his friends became Haldorsson family tales."

When Magnus stopped talking, Leif added, "True ones. Because Kalberg knew about raptors, the Resistance sent him to work with a German officer who was part of the Nazi occupation force. The officer wanted to learn how to hunt with a falcon, so Kalberg taught him."

"And spied on him," said Magnus.

"And spied on him," Leif agreed. "But unexpectedly Bjørn Kalberg and the German officer became friends. The German was an educated man who loved art and music and good writing, and who was glad to be posted to Norway, rather than to a front line where he would have had to do something bad. He lived in the heart of Oslo and loved it. He didn't think of the Norwegian people as his enemies."

This last speech confirmed what Bob had learned about the Wehrmacht – that although a lot of Germans in the Army were ardent Nazis who didn't hesitate to enact Hitler's orders, many didn't like Hitler at all, but were professional soldiers fighting for their country in exactly the same way American soldiers had fought for theirs.

"I just saw a documentary about a plot to assassinate Adolf Hitler which showed that a lot of the plotters were professional soldiers," Bob said. He was going to go on to ask more about Håkon Haldorsson, but suddenly Aunt Mathilda's voice could be heard calling for Jupiter somewhere outside. Every building in the Salvage Yard had an intercom except for Leif and Magnus's workshop; when Aunt Mathilda had first hired the brothers, Magnus had said he couldn't work for her and Uncle Titus if her voice was going to come out of the walls at any moment.

Bob liked Aunt Mathilda, but when she yelled suddenly, out of nowhere, her voice had a strident pitch that could set your teeth on edge. It certainly caught your attention.

"Jupiter, where are you? Are you with Leif and Magnus? Come out from wherever you are!"

Jupiter looked startled, irritated, and abashed in equal measure.

"That's why we're here, actually," he said. "Because Aunt Mathilda wants to know how you're coming along with the quarter-sawn oak dining table."

"We should have it done by the end of the week," Leif said.

"If we don't run into any more difficulties," Magnus said. "We were having trouble with the lathe."

"Turning the legs," Leif said, "but we should be fine."

"If we're lucky," said Magnus.

It seemed to Bob that after an uncharacteristically talkative interlude – and one in which Leif had gotten more serious, and Magnus more cheerful – discussing their carpentry work had brought both of them back to their normal sunny and gloomy personalities.

"I'll tell my aunt," Jupiter said. "Then we're heading to Headquarters. We have plans to make. It was nice meeting you, Freya."

"It sure was," said Pete.

"We'll see you again sometime, I hope," added Bob.

"I hope so, too," said Freya, smiling at Bob.

Freya's interest in him was so intense — and so obvious — that Bob started to feel not just embarrassed but also a bit sympathetic. He knew how it felt to like someone without really knowing if they liked you the same way. Had his interest in Mallory been as obvious to her as Freya's interest in him was to him? He certainly hoped not. And he had to feel kindly toward Freya, since the reason she liked him was that she liked his writing.

"Don't forget your backpack," Magnus said. "Why do you have a pot of Norwegian geraniums next to it?"

"Are those Norwegian geraniums?" Bob asked in surprise. "I didn't know that. My father got them from a woman he works with, and he wanted to pass them on to someone else."

"They're very pretty," said Freya. "We

had some like them in our garden back in Trondheim. I haven't seen them in California before."

"Would you like them?" Bob found himself saying, to his own surprise. "I was going to give them to Aunt Mathilda, but she's already got plenty."

To his even greater surprise, he found himself adding, "The blue of the flowers matches the blue of your eyes!"

Magnus shot him a surprised glance, and even Leif looked slightly startled, but Freya said, "Really?" then came over to take the flower pot out of his hands.

"Thank you," she said, then went to set the pot on a workbench. She touched the plant's petals and fluffed out its leaves, while Bob wondered why he had said what he'd said, and whether he could take it back.

He was glad when Leif suddenly said, "My grandfather was the gardener in the family. After he died, my father was sent some boxes of papers and mementos from his executor in Norway. They included some pressed flowers he'd made when he was young, along with a packet of letters from Bjørn Kalberg and a painting done by another member of the Resistance, a man named Aksel Olsen. The two of them and Grandfather lived in a small town near Oslo."

"Are the letters from Kalberg in Norwegian?" Bob asked.

"Yes," said Leif. "I haven't read them yet."

"Are there letters from Aksel Olsen, too?" asked Pete.

"No," said Magnus gloomily − and this time with perfect justification. "The war did not turn out very well for him. The Nazis caught him. He was shot in 1944."

"Yikes!" Pete said.

A silence fell over the workshop, and then everyone said goodbye. Bob shrugged into his backpack, and Jupiter led the way out into the sunlight.

There, both Jupiter and Pete turned to Bob, Pete grinning at him broadly. Though Bob was still thinking about the Nazi officer who had wanted to learn to be a falconer and the member of the Norwegian resistance who had befriended him, Pete and Jupe were clearly thinking about the way Freya had looked at Bob.

"I don't know if you should have said that about Freya's eyes!" Pete said, kicking Bob's shoe with the toe of his own. "I never knew writing could make someone so irresistible! Though she sure is pretty!"

"She's just a kid," Bob said, slightly embarrassed. "I know she's our age, but she seems much younger than Mallory and Califia. The strange thing is, I had no idea Leif and Magnus even *had* a sister."

"I did," Jupiter said. "Aunt Mathilda told me. But I didn't know their grandfather was a member of the Norwegian Resistance – or that he had a friend with a gyrfalcon. I've never really thought about falconry much, and suddenly I'm running into it twice in one day. And not just because of my fencing lesson at the Center."

"What do you mean?" Bob asked.

"Wait here for a sec. I'll be right back," Jupiter said.

As they passed the Salvage Yard office, he ran in to give his aunt Leif and Magnus's message.

When he got back, Jupiter continued with his explanation.

"When I was at the Center for Falconry and Fencing this morning, I saw a painting of a falconer in the lobby," Jupiter said. "I also met a man named Günther Böhm. A German artist who seems to think he's pretty well known. Have you heard of him?"

"No," Pete said.

Bob shook his head. "Should we have?"

"I don't know," Jupiter said. "According to him, we should. I haven't looked him up yet. I don't even know if there's anything to look up. But he certainly was impressed with himself. He was dressed all in purple and black, and he had very definite opinions about art. Also about falconry. He said he wanted to study it, and implied it wouldn't be hard for him at all – because, as he put it, he already *was* a falconer." Jupiter took an exaggerated pose, his eyes on the heavens. "He said his art was bold and far-sighted. That it looked life in the eye," he added.

"It sounds as if you didn't like him very much," Pete said.

"That is a correct assumption," Jupiter said, "though he did interest me, as a character. He said his grandfather had been in the German army during the Second World War. In the Wehrmacht."

"Maybe he was part of the plot to kill Hitler!" Pete exclaimed.

"I sincerely doubt it," Jupiter said. "When Böhm talked about his grandfather, he called him a Nazi and went out of his way to explain that he himself had been adopted. Come on, let's get to Headquarters and plan our birthday party. And we still don't know how we're going to get to Lyle Smith's the day after tomorrow. Worthington can't take us. And I hate to ask Leif or Magnus again."

"I have an idea," Pete said. "Connor O'Malley's coming down from Auburn for that 4-H conference, and we've already talked about all of us getting together. He's an artist, and you said that the party had something to do with art, right?" He turned to Jupiter.

"Yes," Jupiter said. "But that's really all I know."

"Maybe Connor can take us," Pete said. "I'm sure he'd like to meet Lyle and Cornelius. Do you think they'd mind?"

"They'd be delighted," Bob said. It was a good idea of Pete's, and Bob was looking forward to seeing Connor again.

"Great!" Pete said. "I'll call and ask him when I get home."

That took care of that, Bob thought. He returned, in his thoughts, to the Haldorsson family tale. He wondered what the letters between Håkon Haldorsson and Bjørn Kalberg might contain. He thought it was interesting that the two of them – along with their friend

Aksel Olsen – had not only worked together in
the Norwegian Resistance but had been close
friends. That had made them a little like The
Three Investigators, Bob thought.

3

A Fantastically Cool Coincidence

Two mornings later, Pete sat at the kitchen table with his father, while across the room his mother hummed to herself as she finished cooking a very late breakfast. It was Saturday, and after working all summer as a set construction supervisor on the movie *Bear Valley*, his father would be home for several weeks. In celebration, his mother was making huevos rancheros, and they smelled great!

Pete drummed his fingers in anticipation as he thought about his artist friend Connor O'Malley. The Three Investigators had met Connor during their first case of the summer – when they'd helped him rescue a great horned owl entangled in a net, and later he'd been with them when they discovered a stash of gold nuggets beneath the floorboards of the old Carnegie library he worked in.

Several weeks later, when he and Bob and Jupe were on another case up in the Gold Country, Pete had been gobsmacked when it turned out that Connor was also the 4-H Club sponsor of Jupiter's newly-discovered second cousins, Luke and Harper – who were raising goats.

And on top of all that, Pete had had a great idea for a new logo for The Three Investigators – a chimera – and had asked Connor to design it. Connor was expected in Rocky Beach that very afternoon, and he'd agreed to drive The Three Investigators and Mallory MacLeod to the party at Lyle Smith's house in Sherman Oaks that night.

"Earth calling Pete," his father said.

"What?" Pete said. "Oh, sorry. I was just thinking about Connor O'Malley."

"Well, don't think too hard," his father said. "You might break something."

Pete smiled.

"Almost ready!" his mother Valeria called. She was wearing big hoop earrings and a flowered bandana tied around her forehead to keep her long curly hair out of the way.

"This looks terrific," Martín said as Pete's mother put the plates of corn tortillas, refried beans, fried eggs, and warm homemade salsa down on the table.

"Thanks, Mom!" Pete said. He picked up his knife and fork and dug in. It not only looked terrific; it *was* terrific.

"So you'll be home for how long?" he

asked his father.

"At least two weeks," his father said. He had a dazzling smile, and he flashed it at his wife. "With mi novia."

Pete's mother blushed and swatted Martín's shoulder. Not for the first time, Pete thought that it must have been through her that he'd gotten his propensity to blush easily. His father never blushed.

"I hope you and your friends are taking it easy between now and when school starts," Pete's father said. "You've been awfully busy this summer."

"All work and no play," Pete's mother said, shaking her head.

"I *know*," Pete said, "That's what I keep telling Jupiter." Though actually, he didn't. The last case they had investigated had been solved largely because of his own interest in it.

Pete took a big bite of eggs and refried beans just as the telephone started to ring. His mother looked at his father.

"Are you expecting a call?" she asked. His father shook his head. "Then it's for you, Pete," his mother said.

Pete chewed as fast as he could and then washed down his food with a gulp of milk. He got to the phone just as it finished its fifth ring.

"Hello?" he said.

Jupiter's voice came over the line, and he sounded tense and excited.

"Pete," he said. "I'm at the Center for Falconry and Fencing. Remember that painting of a falconer I told you and Bob about? It's been stolen!"

"Stolen!" Pete exclaimed.

"During the night," Jupiter said. "The police had come and gone before I even got here for my lesson. Nothing else was taken. Nothing was broken. The whole thing is very odd. So odd that I have the feeling this could be the beginning of a very interesting case. Worthington's already with me, and we could drive back to get you and Bob if we have to."

"Maybe my father could give us a ride," Pete said. "He's home for a while. Let me ask him."

He covered the receiver with his palm and yelled to his father. It didn't take long for his father to say he'd be glad to help.

"We'll be there as soon as we can," Pete told Jupiter. "Don't do anything without us."

Pete rushed to finish eating, then took his plate to the sink and rinsed it before putting it in the dishwasher.

"Now, don't stay away all day," his

mother said. "Remember you're going to that party in Los Angeles tonight. Don't wear yourself out."

"Thanks, Mom," Pete said. In the excitement, he'd almost forgotten about the party at Lyle Smith's house. That party involved some paintings, too! he thought.

Happily Bob was home and had no plans, and within fifteen minutes, Pete and his father and Bob were headed for the Center For Falconry and Fencing. When they arrived, Pete thanked his dad, and then he and Bob waved as Mr. Crenshaw drove away.

Pete was impressed by the look of the Center. He had always liked Spanish mission-style buildings, but he had never seen one where the courtyard was placed between two wings.

To the right of the courtyard was a wing with a sign that read "Reception" and to the left was a sign that read "Offices." The courtyard had a high wall, but in the middle, a set of weathered wooden arched double doors stood open at the moment. Through them, Pete glimpsed olive trees, raised planters with flowers, stone benches, wooden tables, and comfortable chairs.

Just then, Worthington and Jupiter

walked through the double doors under the archway. They must have been waiting in the courtyard for Bob and Pete to get there.

Jupiter wasted no time on greetings.

"I'm glad you got here so quickly," he said. "Worthington has managed to secure us an interview with the director, Mr. Hutchinson, but he's busy at the moment with a scheduled appointment. He'll see us when that comes to a close."

"You're terrific, Worthington!" Pete said clapping him on the arm.

Worthington accepted the compliment with a good-natured smile.

"So what happened?" Bob asked.

"I was a little late for my lesson," Jupiter said, "so I just hurried through the lobby and to the locker room to change into my fencing jacket. My instructor didn't mention anything about the break-in, so it wasn't until I'd showered and changed and come back out to meet Worthington that I noticed the painting was missing. When I asked the receptionist, she told me that it had been stolen during the night."

"Wow!" Bob said. "If you hadn't had your first lesson two days ago, you'd never even have known the painting had been there in the first place."

"Where's the crime scene tape?" Pete asked.

"There isn't any," Jupiter said. "The receptionist told me she doubted the police would be taking this very seriously."

"Why not?" Bob asked.

"Because, in the first place, nothing else was taken. It looks like a very targeted theft. Also, although the Center has an alarm system, it wasn't even tripped. And nothing was damaged."

"Do they think it was an inside job?" Bob asked.

"I really don't know what they think," Jupiter said. "It's a very strange place for a robbery, unless you want a lot of foils, épées, sabres, and leather gauntlets. The place just doesn't have anything really valuable in the main building."

"Except that painting," Pete said.

"No," Jupiter said. "That's one of the mysteries. From what I can gather, the painting wasn't all that valuable. In fact, other than the falcons themselves, there's not much of real value in the entire complex."

"So what do we do while we wait for Mr. Hutchinson?" Bob asked.

"The Three Investigators will do what we

do best," Jupiter said. "We'll investigate."

"Do you think we could investigate the mews?" Pete asked. "I'd really like to see the falcons."

"Maybe we can manage that," Jupiter said. "But first I want to look around a bit. I want to see if anything strikes us as curious or unusual."

Even as Jupiter said this, Pete noticed him glance back at the courtyard wall. A wide strip of thick very green grass – kept lush, Pete thought, by hidden sprinklers – ran in front of the wall and the building's two wings.

"What's that?" Jupiter said, pointing to a spot in the grass, then led the way to it. Pete and the others followed, and shortly, the four of them were staring down at a place where the grass had been flattened. Jupiter got down on his knees and parted the grass with his fingers. There were six dimples in the ground, roughly in the shape of a circle. Someone had pushed something into the earth – six times, it seemed to Pete – and as he looked at them, a chill ran down his spine.

His mother was into all sorts of spiritual stuff – some of it quite spooky – and Pete remembered her talking about hexagrams in witchcraft.

"Whoa!" he said. "These indentations could be the outside points of a hexagram! Maybe the painting got taken through some New Age magic!"

Jupiter glanced at him skeptically. "You don't really believe in magic, Pete.

Pete smiled ruefully. "Not *really*," he said.

"Maybe someone had a step stool and put it in front of the wall, to try to climb it," Bob said. "Though a step stool only has four legs. And that wall is so high a step stool wouldn't help much."

"That's true," Jupiter said. "Also, a step stool or a stepladder would have made bigger marks, and the indentations would be slightly slanted. These are absolutely vertical."

Pete nodded. That was the sort of observation that made Jupiter Jupiter. The legs of step stools and stepladders were always angled toward their smaller tops for stability.

"Maybe it has something to do with watering the grass," Pete suggested.

"There's an automatic sprinkler system," Jupiter said. He stared at the indentations as he pinched his lower lip and thought.

"While we were waiting for you to get here, Worthington and I discovered that the Center's security system is rudimentary and controls only the perimeter. The interior doors and windows opening onto the courtyard aren't wired."

"That's a little odd," Bob said.

"Perhaps merely an economic decision," Jupiter said. "But it makes sense when you remember how little of value is here. And the perimeter wall is quite forbidding. Still, it's interesting to note that if someone had been able to get over the wall and into the courtyard, he could have simply strolled into the reception area and taken the painting."

"But how did he get over the wall?" Bob asked. "That stucco is much too smooth for any free climbing."

"And how did he get himself and the painting back out again?" Pete asked. "The wall's so high you'd need a ladder."

"We'll have to answer those questions if we're going to crack this case," Jupiter said, leading the way back into the courtyard. There, Pete saw a long wooden courtyard table placed against the interior wall.

"Look!" he said. "The thief could have stood on that."

"Very observant, Pete," Jupiter said. "You may have solved the problem of how the thief removed the painting. Just a minute."

Without another word, Jupiter dashed across the courtyard and through the door into the lobby. In no time he was back.

"I asked the receptionist if any of the courtyard furniture had been moved, and after she looked out, she told me that one of the small square tables did seem slightly out of place. Perhaps the thief put that smaller table on top of the big wooden one and then was able to climb up and set the painting on top of the wall. After that, he might have climbed down again, set the small table back, then pulled himself up to the top of the wall, lowered the painting on a rope and jumped after it."

"I was wondering how the thief could make sure it wasn't damaged," Bob said. "You've explained how he might have made it back out with the painting. But I still don't see how he made it in. Unless he was a bird, of course!"

Jupiter stared at Bob, nodding. "Or possibly a gymnast," he said. "Perhaps those marks in the soft soil outside the wall were made by the rubber feet of a small trampoline. A gymnast might have leapt onto the trampoline, then vaulted to the top of the stucco wall."

"A gymnast!" Pete exclaimed. "That really might explain it!"

He would have gone on with this line of thought, but just then, a man entered the courtyard who Jupiter seemed to recognize. He was wearing a pair of denim overalls over a white tee shirt. Pete could see he had strong shoulders and beefy forearms, and he settled down at one of the tables and unpacked a paper bag lunch. When he looked up and saw Worthington and the boys, he smiled pleasantly and nodded.

"That's Dave Tyler," Worthington said. "He's been the Center's handyman for ages."

"He's the man who took Günther Böhm – that German artist – on a tour of the Center the other day," Jupiter said. "Let's go talk to him."

As the four of them walked toward him, he smiled more broadly, obviously welcoming them.

"Hello, William," he said to Worthington. "Are these your sons?"

Worthington laughed. "I wish they were," he said. "These boys call themselves The Three Investigators and I work for them from time to time."

Mr. Tyler looked at Jupiter. "You I've seen before," he said. "Are you taking fencing lessons?"

"Yes, sir, " Jupiter told him. "With Mr. Rasmussen."

"One of the best," Mr. Tyler said approvingly. "In fact, if I remember correctly, you were in the lobby with that German fellow who I took on a tour of the place the other morning. Am I right?"

"Yes, indeed," Jupiter said.

"A very strange man," Mr. Tyler said. "Although he was interested in the mews, he also wanted me to take him everywhere else in the Center – down every hallway, behind every door, even into one of the storage rooms at the back. I finally had to tell him I had work to do. He told me *his* work was using bits of other people's paintings to create what he called a 'melange.'"

"Jupiter didn't like him, either," Pete said.

"It's not my place to like or dislike the Center's clients," Mr. Tyler said, "though if I had to choose between having a drink with him and a drink with the lamppost, I'd choose the lamppost. I mean, look at me! And there he was in his purple shirt and black pants and those square glasses. But it takes all sorts to make a world."

"Boys," Worthington said. "Let's let Mr.

Tyler eat his lunch in peace.”

“Sorry, Mr. Tyler,” Pete said.

“Not at all, not at all. I’m pleased to meet you. And good to see you again, William!”

The four of them were walking back in the direction of the lobby when Pete said, “What a nice guy!”

“Yes,” Jupiter said, “and a very even-handed one, too. Bob, have you had a chance to do any research on Günther Böhm?”

“I just began,” Bob said. “I found his website, complete with photos of some of his work, which was very strange. All bits and pieces of things that didn’t match one another, glued together. And with little explanations about what it was all supposed to mean, at-tached here and there. I also found a number of online articles that mention him. But they were all in German and when I tried to trans-late them, some made more sense than others. Anyway, just let me say it seems that no one has a mild opinion about him. Other than Mr. Tyler.”

Worthington checked in with Joanna Schultz and discovered that Mr. Hutchinson would soon be wrapping up his meeting.

“We only have a few minutes,” he said.

"But why don't we take a quick look at the mews? All the instructors are at lunch."

The mews was in the back of the Center's property − a long low building with partitions separating the various falcons who stood tethered to their perches by strips of leather. It was pretty dim inside, and Pete was startled to find that the birds were wearing leather hoods. Even so, they radiated fierceness and keenness. Each of them stood motionless, its claws tightly grasping its perch. Pete thought that if a falconer appeared and removed the hood, the bird would be instantly ready to hunt.

Pete saw that Jupiter didn't really seem interested in the falcons themselves; instead, he was studying a pile of gloves and gauntlets he'd found on a shelf. He was shuffling through them as though he was looking for something.

Bob asked him what he was looking for.

"In the stolen painting, there was a set of initials on the falconer's gauntlet," said Jupiter. "I was wondering if having your initials on your gauntlet was a falconry tradition. It doesn't seem to be. Anyway, I expect the Director's ready for us now."

The Director's office was large and well-furnished, with tall glass doors that opened onto the courtyard. Mr. Hutchinson shook hands with all four of them, exchanged small talk with Worthington, then asked them to have a seat.

"William tells me that you're among the best investigators in California, in spite of your youth," he said. "I'm glad you're on the case."

Jupiter smiled. "The other day when I had my first fencing lesson, I was impressed by the painting and I'm intrigued by its disappearance. Thanks for taking the time to speak with us."

"That's quite all right, Jupiter," Mr. Hutchinson said. "Ask whatever you want."

"To begin," Jupiter said, "do you have any idea why someone would want to steal the painting of a falconer from the Center?"

"None at all," Mr. Hutchinson said.

"Ms. Schultz told me that the Danish actor Per Jorgensen gave it to the Center."

"Yes," Mr. Hutchinson said, "which is why we'd like to get it back. Mr. Jorgensen was very grateful to us for the training we gave him, and we were very grateful to him, as well, for the bequest that accompanied the painting. The painting is more a sentimental reminder of our work together."

"Per Jorgensen?" asked Pete, turning to Jupiter. "You didn't tell us that!"

"I didn't know you knew his name," said Jupiter. "I'd never heard of him before. But Joanna Schultz told me he was a Danish actor who was trained by the Center, and was later nominated for an Oscar."

"For the role in which he used his fencing and falconry training," Mr. Hutchinson said.

"Wow!" Pete said. "My father worked on that movie. It was called *The Seventh Messenger*! Per Jorgensen was great in it!"

As he spoke, Pete suddenly wondered if his father knew Per Jorgensen well enough to ask him if *he* had any ideas about the theft.

Meanwhile, Jupiter was still asking Mr. Hutchinson questions.

"Has there been anything suspicious happening around the Center recently?" Jupiter asked. "Any unusual or unexpected interest in the painting?"

"No," Mr. Hutchinson said. "Nothing at all out of the ordinary. We had the painting appraised when we first received it, for insurance purposes, and we were surprised that its value as a work of art is quite modest."

"But if it had little value, why would someone steal it?" Jupiter asked.

Mr. Hutchinson shrugged. "I have no

idea."

Jupiter pinched his bottom lip again. "I thought the painting was very good," Jupiter said. "I don't understand why its value is so low."

"The value of a work of art is almost always tied to the perceived importance and current reputation of the artist," Mr. Hutchinson said. "In this case, the painting was done by a minor artist whose work is neither well known nor much sought after. Besides, it's not representative of his work."

"What do you mean?" Jupiter asked keenly.

"As I'm sure you'll remember, the painting was highly detailed and very realistic," Mr. Hutchinson said. "The falcon's feathers, for example. The intricate workings on the gauntlet. The jess that attached the falcon to the gauntlet. All very painstaking."

"And why was this unusual?" Jupiter asked.

"Because the artist wasn't a realist," Mr. Hutchinson said. "The appraiser noted that the work deviated from the artist's usual style."

"That's curious," Jupiter said. "I wonder if we might have a copy of the appraisal."

"I'll have Joanna make you a copy before you leave," Mr. Hutchinson said.

"Boy," Pete said. "I wish I'd seen the painting."

"Well, young man," Mr. Hutchinson said. "Perhaps I can help with that."

He opened a drawer in his desk, took out a sheet of glossy paper, and handed it to Pete. It was a high quality reproduction. He looked at it closely. He was astounded at the detail. It was almost spooky, the way both the man and the falcon were ready to stare him down.

Pete showed the reproduction to Bob, then moved to hand it back to Mr. Hutchinson, but the director shook his head. "You boys can keep that," he said. "I have several copies."

"Thanks!" Pete said. "I'm sure this will come in very handy!"

Jupiter asked a few more questions, but none of them led to anything, so he brought the interview to an end.

"Thank you very much, Mr. Hutchinson," he said. "You've been a pleasure to speak with, and we're very grateful for all your help."

Mr. Hutchinson nodded agreeably, then let them out through the doors that opened onto the interior courtyard. It was much warmer in the sun, and after the dimness of

Mr. Hutchinson's office, just a little dazzling. Pete squinted as he stared at the reproduction of the stolen painting. "I see why you liked this, Jupe," he said. "It's really good."

As they walked, Pete turned the reproduction over. The glossy white paper reflected the sun and almost blinded him. He closed his eyes to slits. He could just make out that words had been written on the back in a tiny script. Bright spots floated across his vision. Though he couldn't read them, he suddenly had a hunch the words might prove important, and his heart began to beat a little faster. "Hey, guys," he said. "Come look at this!"

He moved into the shade of the perimeter wall, and Jupiter and Bob crowded next to him. Though the words came into better focus, Pete still found it hard to read the spidery script. "What does it say? I can't read it," he told them.

"Wow!" Bob said, looking closely, his voice rising enthusiastically. "What a fantastically cool coincidence!"

Jupiter looked at the script intently. "It's the title of the painting and the artist," Jupiter said. "The painting is called "Medieval Falconer 4.""

"Four?" Pete said. "What does that

mean?"

"I don't know," Jupiter said. His voice crackled with excitement. "But listen to this. The artist's name is – Aksel Olsen!"

"Aksel Olsen!" Pete said. "That's – !" Pete could hardly find the words. Aksel Olsen was the name of Leif and Magnus's grandfather's friend! The Norwegian Resistance fighter the Nazis had shot!

4

A Second Sighting

About six hours later, Jupiter sat on the edge of the wooden deck in front of the Salvage Yard's Office. Next to him, Bob and Mallory MacLeod talked intently to one another, and Jupiter was glad to have this brief time to himself. The three of them were waiting for Pete and Connor O'Malley to arrive in Connor's car and whisk them off to Sherman Oaks.

Jupiter thrust his hands even more firmly into the pockets of his new khakis, thinking about the day's events and wishing quite hard that he wasn't going to this party tonight at Lyle Smith's. Right now, when events were coming together and the dim contours of a new case were beginning to make themselves visible, he wanted nothing more than to be able to sit quietly and think.

But Bob and Mallory were pleased to be going, so he didn't complain.

Jupiter was glad to finally see Mallory again. Though she'd been working hard at the Salvage Yard since they'd all returned from their Isla Vista adventure, he'd only had a

71

chance to talk with her once since then. His Aunt Mathilda wanted the new Yard website to go live before the end of the summer, and Mallory had been trying to get at least a bit of the inventory from every shed catalogued and listed before that happened.

Listening to Mallory talk to Bob, Jupiter remembered how, at the summer's beginning, he'd been cool and standoffish with this new girl who'd just arrived from Scotland – though over the last weeks, he'd warmed to her considerably.

She'd proven herself invaluable on several of The Three Investigators' cases, and Jupiter had surprisingly keen memories of the two of them breaking into the dilapidated warehouse near Santa Barbara where the stolen capybaras and macaws were being kept, and of them speeding over the water with Rafael Solares toward Catalina Island in pursuit of the kidnappers who'd taken Pete and Bob.

Jupiter had to admit that he'd come to like Mallory a lot. She was smart, focused, courageous and – well – a pleasure to be with. Tonight she was wearing black tights and a blue belted tunic with a floppy neck he thought was called a cowl. She looked very nice. He and Bob were dressed up too, in their new school clothes, and all three of them, he thought, were beginning to look quite grown up. By now, Bob had filled him in on the reason for the fund-raising party at Lyle Smith's house.

It seemed that a Russian-American painter named Evgeni Voronin had painted a series of murals of scenes of Colonial and Revolutionary America in a building that was now a magnet school for the arts in Los Angeles, but although there was common agreement that the paintings were very accomplished, the current head of the school board wanted to paint them over, because he claimed that the paintings of Native Americans and slaves would make current students feel 'unsafe.'

As Jupiter listened to Bob and Mallory talk, he found that they were actually discussing the situation right now.

"So Lyle Smith is hoping to get pledges tonight from artists and dealers and wealthy benefactors," Bob was telling Mallory. "He wants to raise as much money as possible to save the Evgeni Voronin murals. At the moment, this guy named Xavier Coleman is planning to paint over the murals, or to just smash the plaster the paintings are on."

"Good grief," said Mallory. "How can

people be so stupid? But how is money going to stop it?"

"I think Lyle is thinking of using the money for a lawsuit, or even of buying the building outright, if they can raise enough," Bob said.

Just then a battered old sedan swerved through the Salvage Yard's wrought-iron gates, with Pete hanging out of the passenger side window waving happily. "We're here!" he yelled.

Jupiter remembered the car well. He'd gotten into it against his better judgment and then had been taken on a hair-raising ride by Connor O'Malley on his quest to free a great horned owl. As the sedan came to a stop, Pete jumped out hooting. "Mallory!" he yelled. "Bob! Jupe!"

Connor O'Malley got out of his car a bit more sedately. He'd cleaned himself up as best he could, Jupiter saw. He was wearing paint-free dark slacks and a sport jacket over a button-down shirt, but he hadn't managed to entirely get the streaks of paint out of his hair.

"Hello, you three!" he said. "It's been ages!" Everyone crowded around, shaking Connor's hand, patting him on the back, saying how good it was to see him.

It hadn't been ages exactly, Jupiter thought. But it had been almost nine weeks since they'd stood together on the steps of the Auburn library after discovering Li Chang's hidden bag of gold. After that, they'd also seen him at dinner at Jupiter's great-aunt's house in Jackson.

"I remember the way you looked at the library," Connor said to Jupiter. "Arms outstretched, declaiming like a Roman senator. What was it you said? Fortune favors the bold?"

Jupiter smiled and everyone laughed.

"And from what Pete's been telling me," Connor went on, "truer words were never spoken. You four have been bold this summer and you've had a great deal of good fortune! You've solved two more cases since I saw you last, in Jackson. I want to hear all about them. But now get in the car or we're going to be late!"

And they were off. As they merged onto the freeway heading south, Bob asked Connor if he knew Evgeni Voronin's work, or anything about the current controversy, and Connor said he hadn't heard of him until Pete had asked him to come to the party. But he'd now looked up the murals online, and thought he'd been a wonderful painter.

"He was really, really good," Connor said. "The very idea of destroying that splendid work!" He scowled and hit the steering wheel.

Jupiter hadn't known Connor O'Malley long, but he was still surprised about how passionate he seemed about this issue. Just as passionate as he'd been about saving a great horned owl, the day that Jupiter had first met him. It seemed that Lyle and his partner were passionate about it, too, if they really were willing to try to raise enough money to buy a building just to keep the paintings inside it from being destroyed.

Jupiter had only been to Lyle Smith's house once before – in the daytime – when The Three Investigators and Mallory had called on him while searching for a missing tapestry. The house was mostly a glass box, framed by steel posts and girders, with reclaimed redwood siding. At night, with the drapes open, it blazed with light. The party was obviously already in full swing; the living room looked stuffed with people. The pebbled courtyard was illuminated by flickering candle lanterns, and small groups stood talking in the semi-darkness.

The house's front door stood open to welcome partygoers, and the five of them walked in a bit hesitantly. Lyle had pushed the couches and other furniture back against the glass walls to allow more space for standing and mingling. The tall marble display stands Jupiter remembered held brilliant extravagant arrangements of cut flowers, and ceiling-mounted spots illuminated the walls hung with the art Lyle had collected.

What Jupiter saw immediately – what anyone entering would see – was the semicircle of easels on which scaled-down reproductions of the Evgeni Voronin murals had been arranged. Jupiter studied them closely and – as he had at certain times in museums and at the Center when he'd first scrutinized Aksel Olsen's painting – he knew he was looking at true art.

"Can you believe how good these are?" asked Mallory. "Also, Voronin had to work at top speed, right behind the plasterers, while the plaster was still wet."

Jupiter found himself siding more and more with Mallory and Connor in their indignation. All of them were talking about the Voronin paintings when Jupiter felt a tap on his shoulder.

He turned to see the smiling face of Lyle Smith. He was dressed more formally than he had been the first time they'd met – then, Lyle had been barefoot and wearing what had looked like black martial arts pajamas. Tonight he was dressed as the urbane host of a fund-raising party, in an ivory silk suit. He looked delighted to see them, and much younger than his seventy-something years.

Right behind him was a tall, thin man – a bit taller than Lyle and about the same age – whose handsome cinnamon-brown face radiated calm intelligence, self-possession, and something, Jupiter thought, like ironic detachment. He wore no suit but rather a bright poplin shirt the color of California poppies, a light brown vest with hand-carved wooden buttons, blue jeans, and a striking nubbly flat-topped hat shot through with oranges and reds and blues, over an amazing head of short dreadlocks. He looked at Jupiter with gleaming eyes, and Jupiter felt quite drawn to him. He was very cool.

"Welcome!" Lyle Smith said. "I'm so glad you could come. I want you all to meet my partner, Cornelius."

When they'd met Lyle Smith, he'd told them that Cornelius was mixed race – a perfect blend of Samoan Islander, Navajo Indian, African-American, and English.

"Wow!" Pete said, sticking out his hand. "I'm Pete. It's good to meet you. How's your back doing?"

When they'd met Lyle, Cornelius had been in the hospital with disk problems.

"I'm all better until the next time," Cornelius said, chuckling.

Everyone shook his hand and Jupiter was impressed by how he inclined his head and looked attentively at each of them, as if he was really interested in knowing them.

Pete said, "This is our friend, Connor O'Malley. He's an artist! He designed The Three Investigators' chimera logo! But he also does his own work – real work. He's doing paintings of old-fashioned envelopes with old-fashioned stamps!"

"That sounds interesting," Lyle said as he shook Connor's hand. "Should I be collecting your work?"

"I'd highly approve if you did!" Connor replied.

"Mallory, you look lovely," Lyle said, "if I'm allowed to say such things these days."

"You are," Mallory said, smiling.

Lyle turned to Cornelius. "This is the young woman who knew at once that the Frémont quilt tapestry I thought was a reproduction was the original."

"I told Lyle the same thing years ago,"

Cornelius said, "but he wouldn't believe me. And I truthfully wasn't sure myself. You have quite an instinct."

"Though that's really all it is," Mallory said. Jupiter could see she was a bit embarrassed by all the compliments.

"I'm so glad Cornelius is well again," Lyle confessed. "Having him out of the house was a nightmare. When he's not around, I can barely remember my name!"

"When did the two of you meet?" Mallory asked.

Lyle turned to Cornelius. "Why don't you tell them?" he said. "They've already heard enough from me."

It was clear to Jupiter that Cornelius was the less outgoing of the two, but he was happy to tell the story. "We met at an art gallery," he said, "when I was twenty-five and Lysander was twenty-six. I don't know if it was love at first sight, but we certainly recognized each other right away – both of us fanatical about art, both with names we weren't crazy about. We were born in the late forties, when everyone was named Charles or John or Robert."

"We were both named after famous 19th century Americans who many people weren't familiar with," Lyle interjected. "Cornelius

Vanderbilt," he said, pointing at Cornelius. "Lysander Spooner," he said, whacking himself on the chest. "Both admirable men, but such monikers!"

"So we settled on Lyle and Neil," Cornelius said. "And one another."

"Wow!" Pete said. "You've been together a long time!"

"Young man," Lyle said. "If you make another comment about our age, I'll have to ask you to leave the party."

"If I'm remembering correctly, Lyle told us you're an art restorer," Jupiter said. "What exactly does that mean?"

"It means I'm a hermit in a dark cave with small brushes and foul-smelling liquids," Cornelius said deprecatingly.

Lyle laughed. "Neil is a miracle worker! He takes canvases that have been damaged, or that the years have been unkind to, and he manages through alchemy to bring them back to their original beauty. He's the best in the business!" He turned and scanned the room full of guests. "Now where did Matthias get to?" he asked, almost to himself.

"Matthias Mueller," Cornelius explained. "An art dealer friend of ours. His nephew is with him for the summer, and we thought he'd enjoy meeting you."

"There he is!" Lyle said, waving gaily. "This way, young people!"

"You go introduce them," Cornelius said to Lyle. "I'll look after our other guests." He turned to Jupiter and his friends. "It was a pleasure to meet you," he said.

Jupiter found himself being led across the crowded room by Lyle, followed by Bob, Pete, Mallory, and Connor. Soon they were standing in a corner of the room in quite a large circle — the five of them together with Lyle and three strangers. Lyle made the complicated introductions.

Jupiter soon discovered that Matthias Mueller, like his nephew, was German — though he had been in the United States for many years and had had success as an art dealer and gallery owner. He was a cheerful man with expressive eyebrows, bright blue eyes, a shock of blond hair, and a healthy goatee. Jupiter thought he must be in his forties, though he looked younger.

His nephew's name was Werner and although he, too, had blond hair, he had dark brown eyes, very intense. But he smiled easily and clearly had a mischievous side. Next to him was a young woman who Jupiter thought must be in her early twenties. It turned out that her name was Dika Horváth, and that she was from Romania.

Jupiter knew nothing about Romania except that it wasn't all that far from Serbia, where his mother's family had originated. Dika was quite short – not much over five feet tall – with broad shoulders and expressive arms. Her hair was dark, short, and wiry, but the clothes she was wearing reminded Jupiter a little of the clothing worn by their acquaintance Charlotte Mitchell – very bold and colorful and feminine. Apparently she worked in Matthias Mueller's art gallery.

"Now all of you enjoy yourselves," Lyle said merrily. "I'm going to attend to the richer guests."

"Dika walked in one day when I was feeling frantic," Mr. Mueller said after Lyle had gone. "She's wonderful at convincing customers to take the plunge and actually buy a painting they've become interested in."

"It isn't hard to get people to spend money," Dika said. "What's hard is getting the money in the first place! Anyway, I've always loved paintings. Nicolae Grigorescu was one of my favorite painters when I was growing up."

"What kind of work did Grigorescu do?"

asked Connor.

"He knew Renoir," Dika said. "He was sort of a realist, sort of an Impressionist."

With all the noise in the room, it was impossible for them to have one large conversation, so they broke up quite naturally into two smaller groups. Connor and Pete started talking to Dika, while Mallory and Bob talked to Matthias Mueller and his nephew. Jupiter felt caught in the middle, trying to listen to both conversations at once, and having little luck.

This was one of the reasons he disliked large parties — too much noise, too many distractions and fragmented conversations, when he preferred to focus on one thing. He wound up joining the conversation with Mallory, Bob, and the Muellers.

"And that's how I first heard of The Three Investigators," Werner was saying.

That quickly caught Jupiter's attention and, to his amazement, it turned out that, back in Germany, Werner had read an interview in which the French art thief Huganay had credited three American boys he called The Three Investigators with outwitting him. He'd called Jupiter, Pete, and Bob "excellent adversaries, not enemies," Werner explained.

"That's interesting," Bob said. "Because

Jupe is just starting to learn fencing, and he mentioned that being a fencer is a lot like being an investigator trying to outwit an adversary."

He *had* said that, Jupiter thought.

"But now that you mention it," Bob added, "I'm not exactly sure I know the difference between an enemy and an adversary."

"Yes, you do, Bob," Jupiter said. "An adversary is someone you want to defeat – maybe by dueling with them with a foil, and maybe by outwitting them in a case. An enemy is someone you feel you need to destroy."

"That's right," Matthias Mueller agreed. "With adversaries, compromise is not only possible but can be honorable. With enemies, on the other hand, compromise is forbidden, by definition. And I sometimes fear that we're living in an era when people would rather have enemies than friends. When people define themselves by who they hate."

"That's so true," Mallory said. "That's why people like the head of the Bayview High School Board are able to do what they do and get away with it."

Jupiter was struck by the truth of this observation. He was about to add a thought of his own when Bob turned to Werner. "So you've been here all summer?" he said. "Have you learned a lot about the art world?"

Werner started laughing. "I joke with my uncle about this. Mostly I am learning how difficult artists can be — and from working in the gallery I learn how to deal with impossible customers."

"Who has been impossible?" Mallory asked.

"I am thinking of one in particular," Werner said. "I met him not too long after I got to your country. He was completely obnoxious, and unfortunately, he was German, like me and my uncle. I had never heard of this man, though he thought that everyone in Germany must know his name. He had purple shoelaces! And he wore these thick black rectangular glasses that made his eyeballs look like moving paintings!"

Jupiter was sure, from this description, that he knew exactly who Werner was talking about — Günther Böhm! There couldn't possibly be two obnoxious German artists who wore purple shoelaces, he thought.

"Yes," Matthias said. "He was very unpleasant. He was loud and brash and he said the most outrageous things. Oh, how he carried on, bragging about his supposedly cutting-edge work. Cutting is the word for it! He told me he makes collages out of paintings he cuts up and glues to pasteboard! Other people's paintings, you understand. He writes explanations on the pasteboard about what it is all supposed to mean. Then he claimed he would have inherited a painting by Edvard Munch if it hadn't been stolen from his grandfather during the Second World War. He said that if it were ever found and returned to him, he knew just what he'd do with it."

"You won't believe this!" Werner interjected.

"He'd cut it up into little bits and pieces!" Matthias Mueller said in outrage. "He'd shred it in front of a roomful of people and photographers and journalists, and then take the pieces and make them part of whatever horrible stuff he liked to call his 'art'. He had no feeling of sympathy for Munch as a painter – just a belief that this 'sampling,' as he called it, would receive a lot of publicity and be good for his career."

"Boy!" Bob said. "He sounds like a horrible guy!"

"And then he had the cheek to say he wanted to buy one of the works I had on display!" Matthias Mueller went on. "I like to have a small number of representational paintings in my gallery, so long as they are excellent and interesting. I feature contemporary work, especially abstract and nonrepresentational canvases, but when people wander in with different tastes, I like to have something different to show them."

"We don't want to turn anyone away!" Werner said.

"It was strange that the painting he wanted was quite traditional," Matthias said. "He stood in front of it for the longest time and then said how much he disliked it. Was he going to cut that up, too? I wondered. So I told him it wasn't for sale."

"You should have seen his face!" Werner said.

"One must have standards," Matthias Mueller went on, "and I had come to dislike him so much, I refused to let him have the painting. Actually, I'd gotten quite fond of it. It was one of a group of paintings I bought at an auction house in Germany a year and a half ago. I didn't pay much for them — so to be honest I wasn't losing out on a big sale. But they were all quite striking. This one was the last of the lot, and I certainly wasn't going to sell it to that man. I took it home that night. I don't know why, exactly. It's not like anything else in my personal collection."

"Good grief," Mallory said. "Promoting yourself through destroying someone else's art. That's exactly what this L.A. school board is trying to do with the Voronin murals."

"What do you mean?" Werner asked.

"I mean this German artist threatened to destroy a Munch to benefit himself, and this school board is making a name for itself by threatening to destroy Evgeni Voronin's work," Mallory explained.

"And we cannot let that happen!" Matthias Mueller said.

Jupiter decided not to mention to the Muellers that he'd also met Günther Böhm and had had the same reaction to him – if not quite so intense. But then again, Böhm hadn't been threatening to destroy anything the day Jupiter had met him.

He looked up to see Lyle approaching. Lyle announced that the servers had put out food and drink in the dining room, and that he hoped everyone would help themselves. But just then – and somehow not to Jupiter's total sur- prise – he heard a distinctive accent rise above the general clamor of the party, and when he swiveled his head to find its source, he saw the very man they had just been discussing.

Tonight he was wearing orange and purple. His shirt was a blindingly bright orange, his pants were purple and skin-tight, and his pointy black shoes were fastened with orange shoelaces. His black-framed glasses formed a rectangle over his eyes. He was walking next to another man who had also gone out of his way to attract attention with his clothes.

Mr. Mueller had heard him too. "What's he doing here?" Matthias asked Lyle, pointing in Günther Böhm's direction a little rudely. "Did you invite him to your party?"

Lyle followed Matthias's finger with his eyes. "I have no idea who he is. I've never seen him before. He certainly is colorful. But I did invite the man he's walking with. I suppose he's Merrick's guest. Who is he?"

There was no need for Matthias Mueller to answer this question, since right at that moment, Günther Böhm and the man Lyle had called Merrick started making a beeline for where Lyle and Mueller were standing near The Three Investigators. The room was very crowded, and movement from one place to another was difficult, but for reasons Jupiter couldn't have explained, he suddenly hissed at Mallory and Pete and Bob to get away – to go hide themselves in a corner somewhere, so that

Günther Böhm wouldn't see them enough to recognize them again.

Though Mallory looked startled, she and the others did as he asked, so by the time the two newcomers to the party arrived, only Jupiter, Lyle, and Matthias Mueller and his nephew were there to greet him.

"Do my eyes deceive me?" Böhm said, peering at Jupiter. He took off his glasses with a flourish and polished them with a thin black cloth he produced from his shirt pocket. Then he fastened them back in place. "Why, no!" he said. "My vision is perfect as ever. You are the young man I met at that charmingly provincial fencing farm, no? What a surprise!"

Jupiter opened his mouth to speak and then closed it again.

Now Günther Böhm was sticking his hand out toward Lyle. "Merrick tells me you are our host for the evening and a bright star in the constellation of this small part of the world. I am Günther Böhm, *avant garde uber alles*, and I am sure you are delighted to finally meet me." He clicked his heels together and bowed stiffly in Lyle's direction. "Mr. Mueller and I are already acquainted," he said, a grim smile on his thin lips.

Lyle had no choice. He shook his hand

but whipped it back as quickly as he could. "You're a friend of Merrick's?" he said, as if this was difficult to believe.

"Ah, Merrick," Böhm said. "A friend? Well, Günther Böhm has no friends. It is lonely being a visionary, no? So much envy, so much resentment."

The man named Merrick looked uncomfortable – as well he might, Jupiter thought.

"I would like to invite you all to my opening," Böhm said, spreading his arms wide. "I have agreed to lend my celebrity to the New Resistance Co-Op, a fledging outfit with whom I find myself strangely in sympathy. I will be showing some of my recent work – "

"You mean your pasted-together shards of other peoples' art?" Mr. Mueller said derisively.

Böhm smiled as if he had never heard such praise. "When the New appears," he said benignly, "the Old will clash its teeth. But enough about me." He turned squarely toward Lyle. "I am intrigued, Herr Smith, with your desire to save these painted-on-plaster panoramas by the socialist realist Voronin. So two-dimensional and representational, no? I'd have thought you would be more discerning."

Lyle looked seriously offended, but he

was trying to remain polite. "And you, sir?" he asked. "What would you do with the murals?"

"Smash them!" Böhm said gleefully. "And pick up the pieces! I have already contacted the president of the school board to say I would be pleased to help if he will let me select scraps of plaster and carry them away. With those bits and pieces of outdated sentiment, I can build my own honest comments about life!"

Lyle was scanning the room, looking for Cornelius − or maybe a policeman.

"So!" Günther Böhm said. "A memorable meeting! Now do not forget. The New Resistance Co-op, headlined by yours so very truly. When is the opening, Merrick?"

"I −," Merrick said.

"No matter," Böhm said. "It will be in all the papers." He clapped his hands together, as if to perform a magic trick. "Now!" he said. "Refreshments! I am expecting Linzertorte!"

"My, my," Lyle said mildly as Böhm disappeared in the crowd. "I am certainly glad we won the Second World War."

While that was a very clever − and civilized − observation with which to conclude an unpleasant encounter, Jupiter could hardly believe the way Günther Böhm had treated his own host, and as he went off to find Pete, Bob, and Mallory and tell them what had happened, he realized that the mild dislike he had acquired for the so-called artist during their first encounter over art had turned into something a lot darker. He had never liked phonies much, but the phoniness of this particular specimen of the breed was so over-the-top outrageous and unapologetic that Jupiter suddenly half-wished he had committed a crime of some sort so that Jupiter and his friends could bring him to justice.

5

An Auction At Hartung & Hartung

The bright clear morning was still refreshingly cool as Mallory pedaled her bike toward the Salvage Yard the day after the party. The night before, after the unexpected arrival of the bizarre-looking and apparently highly annoying German artist at Lyle Smith's fund-raising party, Jupiter had asked her if she wanted to join him and Pete and Bob this morning to do some research about a Norwegian painter named Aksel Olsen.

Mallory already knew – from Bob telling her about it earlier that day – that Aksel Olsen had been the man who painted the painting that had been stolen from the place where Jupiter was taking fencing lessons, but Jupiter had told her that he'd also been a friend of Leif and Magnus's grandfather, and had been executed by the Nazis.

Jupiter had said "About ten," and punctuality was a virtue to Jupiter – and to Mallory as well. She didn't want to disappoint him, and she was also glad to get away from the apartment she shared with her mother and back to the place she was starting to think of as her second American home.

Mallory loved her mother, but she'd never been as close to her as she'd been to her father, and ever since she'd gotten back from the town of Isla Vista – where she'd joined The Three Investigators on what had turned into an unexpected escapade – her mother had been getting on her nerves.

Although she had explained to her that she had never been in any danger – that only Pete and Bob had been kidnapped, while she and Jupiter had followed safely after them in a second boat – her mother seemed unable to get over her alarm that what she'd been told would be a simple boat ride, camping trip, and cookout had turned into something very different. Nothing like this had ever happened in Scotland! her mother had pointed out.

Good grief, Mallory thought, as she wheeled her bike through the wrought-iron gates of the Salvage Yard. When she arrived, Jupiter and Bob were waiting for her in The Three Investigators' outdoor workshop. They looked up expectantly as she walked in with her laptop in a messenger bag slung across her chest.

Mallory was always glad to see Bob,

who had become a true friend, and she was pleased that Jupiter had asked for her help. In Isla Vista, she and Jupiter had climbed through the window of a warehouse together – discovering smuggled birds and animals inside – and had shared the adventure of pursuing Pete and Bob across the Channel Islands.

But although those experiences had been gratifying, she hadn't done much overall to help to solve The Three Investigator's last case. She hoped she could do better with this new one. Unfortunately, having missed the meeting at the Center For Falconry and Fencing where the boys had made deductions about the theft, she was already a bit behind. Still, she was ready to get focused on the job at hand.

"Hey, Mallory," Bob said. "Have you recovered from last night yet?"

"Not exactly," Mallory said. "I woke up still thinking about the Voronin murals and the idiot who wants to destroy them. Where's Pete? I thought he was going to be here, too."

"His father took him shopping for school clothes," Jupiter said. "Better him than me. I don't enjoy shopping. Particularly not for clothing."

Mallory smiled. "Why am I not surprised?" she said. She sat down in one of the green metal chairs that looked as if they'd been purchased from a classic old motel and opened her laptop – which she hadn't opened since before she'd left her apartment the evening before. At the time, she'd been researching Evgeni Voronin, and as her browser opened to an image from one of the contested murals, a current of incredulity again surged through her.

To Mallory, almost anything made by human hands was to be treasured, and when it came to the work of a real artist, even more so. Even simple crafted items were a pleasure to examine and handle, and she was always happy to find something unique when she was working at the Salvage Yard. However, what Mathilda and Titus Jones had in their Yard was nothing compared to these murals. Anyone wishing to destroy them was a criminal, Mallory thought.

"Do you think Lyle and Cornelius will really be able to save these?" she asked Bob, nodding toward the image on her laptop.

"I don't know, but I hope so," he said. "Unfortunately, the urge to destroy art is nothing new. The other night my father and I saw a documentary about a German plan to assassinate Hitler, and I learned that in the 1920s the

Nazi Party banned what they called 'degenerate art' in Germany."

"How did they ban it?" Mallory asked.

"Well, they couldn't, really," Bob said. "People kept painting what they wanted. But once the war started, they burned some work by very famous artists, and before that, they gathered some of it and held a big exhibition to ridicule it. Since the people who came to see it liked it, that didn't work very well! Also, though the regime officially hated modern art, several of its highest ranking members made off with works to put in their personal collections."

"What a bunch of hypocrites!" Mallory said. "Connor O'Malley was right. The idea of censoring art − . You'd think the Los Angeles school board would be embarrassed to follow the Nazis' example."

"You *would* think so," Jupiter said. "But instead, they might well be quite eager to cooperate with that charlatan Günther Böhm. In fact, I'm afraid they might see his sudden interest in disposing of the plaster pieces of a once-fine work of art as a godsend. Publicity of that kind might give uninformed members of the public the impression that there had really been nothing wrong with what the School Board did."

"What was the guy like when you met him at the Center For Falconry and Fencing?" Bob asked.

"Well," said Jupiter, "he was unbelievably pompous, but he also tried to ingratiate himself to me."

"Did he say anything to *you* about cutting up paintings?" Mallory asked. "Or Edvard Munch?"

"No," Jupiter replied. "Although he mentioned that his father had had a large collection of what he called 'pretty paintings.' He said his grandfather had had some, too."

"What did he mean by 'pretty paintings'? Mallory asked.

"He seemed to think that the painting of the falconer was boring because it was realistic," Jupiter said, "even though he claimed to want to study falconry and said he felt he already *was* a falconer. Because his art supposedly looks life in the eye."

"It doesn't, though," Bob said. "His art looks life in the armpit. It's a horrible mishmash of nothing. Edvard Munch, on the other hand, was an amazing artist. Do you know anything about him, Mallory?" Bob asked.

"Not really," Mallory said.

She opened her laptop, typed *Edvard*

Munch into the search engine, then hit Images, and as soon as she saw a photograph of the painting called *The Scream,* she knew why the name had been familiar. She clicked on some of his other paintings and was surprised at their variety. Some were in bright happy colors, others in dark and gloomy ones, and as she studied the images, she began to decipher a pattern.

"Look how different these are from one another," she said, holding up her laptop. "When you examine the dates, you can see how Munch was changing styles as an artist as he went along."

Bob nodded in agreement.

"And look!" Mallory said. "Here's a Munch painting listed as 'missing.' It was stolen during the Second World War. Maybe it's the one Böhm is threatening to shred, if he ever gets his hands on it."

She clicked on the thumbnail and the browser opened a much larger image of the painting, a color photograph taken in the 1930s. The painting itself dated from 1880. It was a pastoral landscape of a small town, with a village church high on a hill, painted in bright colors.

Mallory thought it was gorgeous.

"Can you believe this?" she said to the others, showing them the painting. "We can't let that madman get his hands on this!"

"Well, he doesn't have his hands on it yet," Jupiter said, "and if it's missing, I don't know how he ever can."

That was true, Mallory realized. In fact, the painting had probably been destroyed long ago. If it hadn't, then by now it would almost certainly have resurfaced from wherever it had been hidden after it was stolen. For her to get upset at the prospect of something being destroyed which had probably *already* been destroyed was a waste of energy. Better to focus on the still-existing Voronins than an already-lost Munch. Better still to focus on the reason she was here this morning, she thought.

"You're right," she said to Jupiter. "Anyway, you said you want to find out as much as possible about Aksel Olsen and why someone might have stolen that painting from the Center."

"Yes," Jupiter said. "Let's get started. Before we do, though, I'd like to find a photograph of a mini-trampoline online."

"Why?" asked Mallory.

"Because there were marks in the grass outside the perimeter wall at the Center for

Falconry and Fencing. Vertical marks, in a circle, like the marks of legs. I hypothesized that a gymnast had used a mini-trampoline to vault to the top of the wall."

Mallory plugged the appropriate search term into her search engine and was offered a number of photographs. She showed them to Jupiter and Bob, and they both nodded.

"That must have been what happened," Bob said. "Geez, Jupiter, what a great deduction. Now, if only we knew how to find the gymnast! At least we can look up Aksel Olsen."

With that, Bob and Mallory both began to do research on their laptops. The initial searches were frustrating, since all the links seemed to lead to documents written in Norwegian.

"How do we find out what these websites really say?" she asked, after trying and failing to get a good translation.

"We could ask Leif and Magnus," Bob said. "Or their sister Freya. They all speak and read Norwegian."

"I still can't believe they have a sister and never mentioned her," Mallory said. Bob had told her about meeting Freya, and she supposed that sooner or later she'd meet her too.

"You know Leif and Magnus," Bob said, shaking his head.

Mallory returned to her computer search. Beyond the Norwegian sites, there just wasn't very much to discover. Olsen had died young – before he had found a mature style – and there were relatively few known canvases. As well, he had died over seventy years before.

"Anything?" Jupiter asked.

"Not much," Mallory said.

"Wait!" Bob said. "Here's something. It's a mention of an auction of ten works by Olsen that took place a year and a half ago. Let me click on this link – " Mallory closed her laptop and went to stand behind Bob. She peered over his shoulder as he opened the home page of a German auction house.

"Hartung & Hartung, in Berlin," Bob said.

"That's interesting," Jupiter said. "Why would a little-known Norwegian artist come up for auction in Germany?"

Mallory ran her eyes swiftly over the page Bob had opened. "Click on that," she said, pointing to a link that read 'Minor Work Twentieth Century.' When Bob did as she asked, she quickly saw another link for 'Olsen, A.'

The page opened to ten thumbnails. Jupiter had joined her now, standing beside her looking over Bob's shoulder. The paintings all seemed to be different sizes and shapes, but they were similar in their colors and their overall impression. Then, one by one, Bob opened the thumbnails in new tabs.

"Wow!" Jupiter said, and that was all.

Rarely, Mallory knew, was Jupiter without words.

Mallory looked carefully at the images as Bob clicked first on one and then the next. Although some of the paintings seemed more vertical than horizontal, and some of them were larger than others, in each one a medieval falconer stood, his arm outstretched, his elbow horizontal to the ground. A falcon perched on the man's wrist. But the landscape in the background of each painting was different, as was the man's costume and his glove and gauntlet. Sometimes the falconer faced the viewer and sometimes he glanced to the right or left.

"It looks as if the falconer in all ten paintings is the same man," Mallory said.

"That's the one that was stolen," Jupiter said, pointing to one of the images on Bob's screen. "The one I saw at the Center. Does it say who the owner was or where the paintings came from?"

"No," Bob said. "But do artists usually paint the same painting over and over again?"

"Well, it isn't the same painting exactly," Jupiter said. "There are subtle differences."

"Also, some pretty obvious ones," said Mallory. "Not to mention that the canvases are all different sizes and shapes."

"Just a minute while I get out the photograph that Mr. Hutchinson gave us," Jupiter said. "Mallory hasn't seen it yet."

He went over to a pile of papers on his chair, and from a folder he pulled out the photograph of the stolen painting. He showed it to Mallory, and then they all compared it to the other paintings on Bob's screen.

"That's strange," Jupiter said. "The gauntlets and gloves the man is wearing are different in each painting, and each has different initials on it."

Mallory looked more closely. Jupiter was right. Her eyes moved from painting to painting. GK, HT, BW, EM, PN, JZ.

"I wonder what they mean," Jupiter said. "I originally thought that the initials were the falconer's, but if the same man is pictured in every painting, then the initials clearly can't be his."

"I wonder who the falconer is," said Mallory.

"I don't know," Bob said, "but here's what we know so far: The painter is Aksel Olsen, a Resistance fighter. One of his paintings was given to Leif and Magnus's grandfather, also a Resistance fighter. And they had a friend who was both a Resistance fighter and a falconer – a man named Bjørn Kalberg. Could Kalberg have been the model for the paintings?"

Mallory and Jupiter both looked at Bob with admiration.

"That is excellent thinking, Bob," said Jupiter. "An excellent hypothesis. See if you can find a picture of Bjørn Kalberg."

As Mallory watched, Bob set to work. His fingers flew, trying one keyword after another, with no luck. All the Bjørn Kalbergs he found were clearly someone else. But when Bob plugged in "World War II Norwegian Resistance," he discovered a site dedicated to the men and women who had been resistance fighters.

There was a long list, and Bjørn Kalberg's name was on it. At the bottom of the page was a link entitled Photographs, and Bob clicked on it. As Mallory watched, Bob scanned through an entire gallery of photos, reading the captions, looking for Kalberg's name.

"Bingo," Bob said, and clicked on a photo. Three tall and rugged-looking men in snow boots and heavy jackets stood with their arms around each other, smiling at the camera. "Kalberg's the one in the middle," Bob said.

Mallory looked at the photograph closely. Bingo, indeed. There was no question that the man in the paintings was this man, Bjørn Kalberg − both the photograph and the paintings showed the same high cheekbones, same square chin, same piercing eyes. Next to him on the left was Aksel Olsen.

He, too, was handsome, though he looked a little shyer − more like the artist he had been. As Mallory stared at his face, she thought of the conversation at Lyle and Cornelius's party, about the difference between an adversary and an enemy. This man had been executed − or murdered − because the Germans occupying Norway had considered him someone who needed to be destroyed.

Or some of the Germans, anyway, Mallory thought. Probably not the German officer who had become friends with Bjørn Kalberg. Bob had told her that the German officer was an educated man who loved art and music and good writing, and who was glad to be posted to Norway, rather than to a place where he might have had to fight and kill.

The two men – one Norwegian and one German – had been able to see beyond the enmity of their countries, to understand who each one had been, as an individual.

Though Mallory felt sad that Aksel Olsen and others like him had been killed for standing up to the Nazis when they occupied his country, she also felt proud of him, somehow.

Bob clearly felt the same way Mallory did. "Aksel Olsen looks like a really great guy," he said.

"Indeed he does," Jupiter agreed. "And the third man in the photograph is almost certainly Leif and Magnus's grandfather – who we know from talking to Leif and Magnus bequeathed an Aksel Olsen painting to their father when he died."

"Leif and Magnus's father has a painting by this artist?" Mallory asked. "I didn't know that. I wonder what *their* painting is of?"

"When they get here, we can ask them," Bob said. "They're due any time now. In fact, I think they're late."

"We can also ask them more about the German officer who wanted to learn falconry, and who Kalberg was sent to spy on," Mallory said. "For example, what was the officer's name, and did he live through the war?"

"Leif didn't say," said Jupiter. "But if they know, we'll find out soon enough. By the way, Mallory, I've been meaning to ask you to our birthday party. I'm the host this year but we're going to have it at the city park."

"What do you mean you're the host?" Mallory asked curiously. "And what do you mean by 'our' birthday party?"

Jupiter and Bob both started to answer at once, but just then there was a bang and a rattle, a swish of sprayed gravel, and a whoop – but the newcomer wasn't Leif or Magnus.

Mallory could see Pete was in a hurry. He jumped off his bike and before he could lean it against the office, it clattered to the ground. He picked it up, seemed to shake it, nudged the kickstand, and settled it in place, then turned and sprinted toward the outdoor workshop.

"Guys!" he yelled. "Oh, hi Mallory!"

He was flushed from the ride over, which Mallory could see he'd done at top speed. His hair was wind-blown, his shirt untucked, and he was a little out of breath. He threw himself into a chair with the others.

"Whew!" he said. "What did I miss?"

"We found out that Aksel Olsen painted not just one, but *ten* paintings featuring a falconer and a falcon, and it seems that the model for the falconer in all of the paintings was the Norwegian Resistance fighter Bjørn Kalberg," Jupiter told him. "The ten paintings were sold at auction in Germany two years ago."

Pete's mouth dropped open.

"One of the ten is the stolen painting," Bob added. "But Jupiter was just inviting Mallory to our birthday party when you skidded in."

This got Pete's attention, too. He sat up, grinning. "It's going to be great this year! Did they tell you that when we first met in kindergarten, we discovered that our birthdays are all within six weeks of one another? Jupiter's is first, on August 18th; Bob's is September 10th, and mine is October 3rd. So we decided to have one party for all of us. When's *your* birthday?"

"November 10th," Mallory said.

"So you're the youngest!" Pete said. "And you're a Scorpio, I think! My mother knows a lot about astrology – well, she knows a lot about all sorts of stuff – but when she explained to me about Jupiter, Bob, and me, it all made sense. Jupe's a Leo, which totally fits since he's First Investigator. He's a natural leader, but he also works well with others."

"Pete!" Jupiter said, clearly embarrassed.

But Mallory could see that Pete was on the Astrology Train and nothing was going to deter him.

"Bob's a Virgo," Pete said. "He's detail-oriented and well-organized. Which makes sense, because he's Records and Research. I'm a Libra," Pete went on, "though sometimes I think that my mother must have gotten my birthday wrong. Libras are supposed to be balanced and like peace and quiet."

"And everyone knows that Pete's the opposite of that," Bob said.

"Well," Pete said. "I like to balance on my bike."

Everyone laughed at that one.

"O.K., you guys," Pete said. "I can't keep this under wraps any longer. I had a great idea about our new case. I mean, no one has asked for our card yet, and no one has hired us – or even said they want to! – but if we're going to squeeze another case in before high school starts, it's pretty much *got* to be this one."

"We're listening," Jupiter said. "Go ahead."

"When my dad and I were out shopping this morning, he asked me what we were doing these days, and I reminded him about the painting that was stolen from the Center. I also told him that the painting had been given to the Center by Per Jorgensen. Remember, in Mr. Hutchinson's office I told you guys that my dad had worked on *The Seventh Messenger?* – the movie Jorgensen was nominated for the Oscar for? So my dad got to know Mr. Jorgensen a little. They're not friends, or anything, but they know each other."

"And?" Jupiter said.

"And," Pete went on, excitedly. "I told my dad that I wished we could interview Per Jorgensen to see if he had any ideas about why the painting he donated had been stolen, or give us any other information that might help. Well, you know how my dad has gotten more and more interested in what we do ever since he got us involved in that case with Daniel Hernández and Phillipa Paxton and that crazy bear-doctor."

"Out with it, Pete," Bob said. "Tell us!"

Pete jumped to his feet and smacked his hands together. "So I asked my father if he could call Mr. Jorgensen and set up a meeting with him!"

"A great idea, Pete," Jupiter said. "I don't know what exactly we would ask him, but perhaps Mr. Jorgensen can help us."

"Perhaps!" Pete yelped. "Of course he can!"

"Good going, Pete," Bob said.

"But that's not all," Pete said. "I took a chance, even though I didn't know everyone's schedule. So my father called Mr. Jorgensen just before I got on my bike to come over here. And Mr. Jorgensen picked up! And we've got an appointment to meet him at his house tomorrow!"

"Wow"! Bob said.

"That's excellent," said Jupiter.

But while this comment didn't surprise Mallory in any way – after all, she thought it was excellent, too – what *did* surprise her was that Jupiter then looked at her and said, "We'll all go, I hope. But Mallory hasn't told us whether she'll be coming to our party."

"I wouldn't miss it for anything," Mallory said – and meant it.

6

Freya Tenders An Invitation

Bob was delighted. He'd been meaning to ask Mallory to the party ever since he and Pete and Jupiter had planned it, but it hadn't come up at Lyle and Cornelius's house, and this morning all the talk had been about art and artists.

Bob sometimes found it frustrating that when he and Mallory were together, they were mostly also with Pete and Jupe. In fact, he'd been wanting to ask her for several days now if she'd like to go climbing again at Palisade Point – partly because she'd decided that she wanted to pick climbing as her special sport in high school, and partly because the last time they'd gone climbing, they'd had an interesting discussion about writing.

Although Bob wasn't yet positive that the stolen painting would actually *be* a case – as Pete had mentioned, no one had asked for their card yet! – he couldn't help but think it would. If it did, he knew already that the noun in the title would be either Falconer or Falcon. After all, they'd already reached the letter "F" in his alphabetical titles, so "falconer" was a no-

115

brainer.

However, until the case evolved a little further, he wouldn't have any idea what the adjective might be, and all he could come up with were words like "fake" or "fabulous" or "fantastic."

Still, the largest problem was that they didn't really know what this case was even *about*. Except, maybe, a gymnast, who, for some strange reason, had used a mini-trampoline to vault a wall around a courtyard so that he could steal a painting of a falconer holding a falcon. And why would he want to do that?

Just then, one of the Salvage Yard's trucks drove through the wrought-iron gates and parked by the Office, backfiring once as the engine was turned off. Pete jumped to his feet, and soon Bob, Jupiter, and Mallory were following him across the gravel to greet the Haldorsson brothers as they emerged from the truck.

Leif clambered down from the driver's seat, while Magnus got out of the passenger side – followed by their sister Freya. When she saw Bob, she smiled and waved. He found he was pleased to see her, and smiled and waved back.

"Good morning!" Leif called out.

"Jupiter, don't tell your aunt we're late!"

"My lips are sealed," Jupiter said.

"Freya, you've met the boys," Leif said. "This is Mallory MacLeod, their friend we told you about. Mallory, this is Freya, my sister. Magnus and I are helping her make a hand-loom."

"Hello," Mallory said. She stepped forward and shook Freya's hand. Freya smiled a bit nervously, Bob thought – but she looked Mallory straight in the eye.

"So you're a weaver," Mallory said. "Just like the goddess you're named for."

Although Mallory didn't seem to think this was a particularly brilliant comment, Freya obviously did.

She stared at Mallory in amazement. "Do you play 'Odin's Hammer' too?" she said.

"What's 'Odin's Hammer'?" Mallory asked.

"It's an online role-playing game for people interested in Norse mythology," said Freya. "We have a Facebook group, too."

"I don't play computer games," Mallory said, dismissively.

Bob knew she disapproved of them on principle, but Mallory's tone softened as she looked at Freya's disappointed face.

"I read books," she explained. "Also, I grew up in Scotland, so I learned a lot about Norse culture. The Vikings were in Scotland by the end of the 9th century."

"Really?" Freya said. "I didn't know that."

Magnus spoke up. "Yes, you did," he said. "When you were five – before we moved to California – we all took a trip to the Orkney Islands."

"You've been to Orkney?" Mallory said, with pleasure. "I've been there, too. I loved it. Anyway, the Scots and the Vikings intermarried – and not just in Orkney but all over northern Scotland. You can find Scottish clans with direct Norse descent. Clan MacLeod is one of them, actually."

Bob had wondered how Mallory and Freya would get along. He'd seen right away that, aside from the fact that they were both immigrants to the U.S., they might not have that much in common, but as Mallory tried to find a way to relate to Leif and Magnus's sister, he admired both her honesty and her kindness. The morning sunlight shone on her red hair, which seemed to glow. He was amazed again at how vivid and intense she was. Next to Mallory, Freya Haldorsson, with her high coloring and her white-blond hair, seemed a bit pale.

But though she lacked Mallory's fire, Freya was clearly interested in pleasing other people, and – trying to follow Mallory's example and be nice to Freya – Bob asked her, "Did you find a place for the geraniums?"

"Oh, yes," Freya said, with a big smile. "I put them in a sunny place in the garden. They're beautiful."

"What geraniums?" Mallory asked. "Those big red flowers?"

"No!" Freya said. "These are small and delicate and blue."

"My father – " Bob began before Jupiter cut him off.

"Pete, Bob, and I – and Mallory – are investigating the theft of a painting," Jupiter said to Leif. "It was hanging on the wall at the place I'm taking fencing lessons, but someone stole it two nights ago. Interestingly, it was painted by Aksel Olsen, your grandfather's friend."

Magnus looked alarmed, Bob thought, but then just about everything alarmed Magnus.

"That's very strange," Leif said. "We did not know his work had gotten beyond Norway."

"It has," Jupiter said. "And now we're wondering about the painting your father inherited. Could you tell us what it looks like?"

"Sure!" Leif said. "It's a portrait of my grandfather's friend Bjørn Kalberg. I remember it hanging on the dining room wall in our grandfather's house. It seemed to mean a lot to him."

"A wonderful painting," Magnus said. "Very gloomy! Kalberg was dressed in clothing from the old days."

Wow! Bob thought. It sounded like another falconer painting!

"Do you know how your grandfather originally got it?" he asked. "We've just discovered that ten of Olsen's works were consigned to a German auction house. Could your grandfather have bought it from the man who later sold the others?"

"Oh no," Leif said. "It belonged to Bjørn Kalberg himself, and he left it to Grandfather in his will."

"You said Kalberg was dressed in clothing from the old days," Jupiter said. "Bob, could you show Leif and Magnus what we found?"

Bob had brought his laptop with him, so he opened it to the page that had the thumbnails of the auctioned Olsen paintings. In the bright sunlight near the Office, they were hard to see.

"Maybe we should go inside to look at these," Bob said.

From behind them there was the bang of a door shutting and the sound of Jupiter's aunt talking to Jupiter's uncle. Any moment now, Mathilda and Titus Jones would come through the gate separating their house from the Salvage Yard.

"We had better get to our workshop before your aunt sees us!" Magnus said to Jupiter. "You can follow us there. Come on, you two."

He grabbed Leif and Freya by the shoulders and hurried them toward the shed where the brothers worked. They had just managed to get the door shut behind them when Aunt Mathilda and Uncle Titus came up on their way to the office.

"Now what are the four of you doing standing here looking like you're searching for the Lost City of Gold?" Mathilda said. "If you don't have better things to do, I have a list of chores as long as my arm!"

"That's O.K.," Jupiter said, backing away. "We need to consult with Leif and Magnus about something."

As Aunt Mathilda and Uncle Titus mounted the steps to the office, Jupiter led the way to Leif and Magnus's workshop. Inside, they found that Leif had lifted the clipboard holding the Haldorssons' work record off the wall, and Bob saw Leif glance at his watch and sign them in, then hang the clipboard up again.

Leif grinned when he saw Bob watching.

"When Mrs. Jones sees this month's time sheet, she won't be as upset that we got here late today as she would have been if she had known about it right away. Now, you can show me the web page."

Bob put his computer down on a nearby work table, and all of them crowded around it, except for Mallory and Freya, who hung back.

"Come look at this," Bob said. "Does your parents' painting look like any of these?"

Leif looked, then started laughing.

"Does it look like any of them?" Leif said. "It looks like all of them. I thought Grandfather's portrait was one of a kind!"

"Why would Bjørn Kalberg stand with a bird on his arm eleven different times?" Magnus wondered. "It seems a strange thing to do."

"Perhaps Aksel Olsen used him as a

model once or twice and then was able to paint the others without him being there," Jupiter mused. He pinched his lower lip. "But why would he do that?"

Everyone looked as though he or she had no idea. Bob certainly didn't. But he said, "We also wanted to ask you about the German officer in your grandfather's family tale. You said that he and Bjørn Kalberg had become friends. Do you know any more about him?"

"What his name was, or whether he lived through the war?" Mallory added.

Magnus said, "I don't think Grandfather ever said what his name was. Did he, Freya?"

"He didn't to me," Freya said. "But he did say the German officer had died in Norway, at the end of the war. He said he was buried in Oslo, and that he had visited his grave."

"Visited his grave?" Jupiter asked, in surprise. "Then your grandfather must have respected him, the way Bjørn Kalberg did. You only visit the grave of someone you respect."

"Unless you go *to dance on it*," Leif said, smiling. "When I was studying English expressions, I learned that one."

"Did you all learn English when you were still in Norway?" Pete asked.

"Ja, selvfølgelig," Leif said, "men vi snakker fortsatt fremdeles norsk."

Magnus laughed.

"He said we all still speak Norwegian," Magnus said. "Though not all the time, of course. The only other thing Grandfather told us about the German was that he had a special role as a cultural liaison officer. He came early in the occupation, and because of his knowledge of music and dance and art and writing, he was supposed to impress the upper class of Oslo and win them over."

"That's right," said Leif. "Grandfather told us that because, by that time, falconry was a sport of the elite, the German officer decided to learn it to better ingratiate himself with the Norwegian upper classes. I remember him telling us that story while we were walking in one of Trondheim's parks."

"Do you miss Norway?" Mallory asked.

"Just sometimes!" Leif said, laughing. "It's an old, old country, and this is a pretty new one. I miss the history that's everywhere you turn there."

"I miss that, too," said Mallory. "After growing up in Scotland."

"Why did Germany invade Norway and Denmark, anyway?" Pete asked. Bob didn't know exactly who Pete was asking, but even so, he was surprised when it was Mallory who answered.

"I think because Norway gave Germany easy access to the North Atlantic – to Scapa Flow, among other things," Mallory said.

"What's Scapa Flow?" asked Pete.

"A gigantic natural harbor," Mallory said. "In the Orkney Islands we were talking about earlier. During the Second World War, the British Navy was based there. The Admiralty thought it would be safe, but at the beginning of the war, a German U-boat got in, sank a battleship, then made it back to Germany. In Orkney, it's a famous story."

"Wow!" Pete said admiringly – not of the U-boat, apparently, but of the fact that Mallory had known the answer to his question. "I guess that's what you mean about history! Though California is also pretty old, when you go back to the Spanish conquistadors. It's amazing how much of history ends up being about war and conquest."

Bob nodded. "That's really true," he said. "But a lot of it is also about art and music and literature. We have to remember that. And when you think about it, artists – and I mean all kinds of artists, like musicians and filmmakers and writers – are the people who create and preserve a culture. That's why what Lyle and Cornelius are doing is so important."

He looked at Mallory and was happy to see her look back at him in fierce agreement.

"In any case," Jupiter said, "this has been a remarkably enlightening morning. We've found out far more than I had expected to. Let's see." He counted on his fingers.

"First, we discovered that the painting stolen from the Center for Falconry and Fencing is one of ten very similar paintings by Aksel Olsen.

"Second, that the subject of all ten paintings is Håkon Haldorsson's friend, Bjørn Kalberg.

"Third, that there's an eleventh painting much like the others, and that it's owned by Leif and Freya and Magnus's father.

"Fourth, that all the paintings except for the Haldorsson painting were sold at a German art auction a year and a half ago."

"Unfortunately, we have no idea where any of the Hartung & Hartung paintings are now," said Bob.

"Also," Mallory said, "the multiple paintings of one subject don't make that much sense, at least to me. Granted, the paintings aren't identical, but I don't think it's common for an artist to paint such a similar painting eleven times."

"I agree," Bob said. "I guess artists sometimes do studies – paintings or drawings of part of a larger work, for practice. But all eleven paintings are complete in themselves. They're not practice for something else."

He paused for a moment and then went on. "When I'm writing up our cases for the website, I may do several drafts – each one different from the others – but with a lot of things in common. Even so, I only publish the final one – I don't put up all the drafts to let readers compare them."

"I don't know if that's a perfect analogy," Jupiter said. "But I get your point. So unless Aksel Olsen was an obsessive who felt compelled to paint the same thing over and over, perhaps there's another reason he did what he did."

"He painted them during the war," Mallory said. "Do you think they could contain secret messages? You remember I told you I wanted to be a code-breaker when I was a kid!"

"That's an intriguing suggestion," Jupiter said, "but we would have to study the paintings very carefully to see if there was any way they could be communicating something."

"What about those letters on the gauntlets?" Bob asked.

Jupiter pinched his lip and looked thoughtful.

"An ingenious supposition. But it hardly seems like an economical way to get a message to anyone. Can you imagine how long it took Olsen to paint those paintings? There had to be easier ways to get even secret messages delivered," he said.

"Maybe there are secret messages hidden in the box of stuff my father got from my grandfather's executor," Freya said suddenly.

"What box of stuff?" asked Mallory with interest.

"When he sent the painting of Bjørn Kalberg to my father, Grandfather's executor also sent some pressed flowers, those skeins of wool for me, and a bunch of letters Kalberg wrote to Grandfather and the letters Grandfather wrote back," Freya explained. "Maybe they wrote something about the paintings to one another. Maybe there's a clue somewhere in the letters that would help you understand why Olsen painted eleven paintings so much alike."

"That's possible," Mallory said. "Though if the letters were written during the war, I'm sure they had more urgent things to write about – and they would have had to be very careful about how they wrote. I bet a lot of letters in Norway were opened and read by the Nazis."

"That's probably true," Freya said, a little crestfallen.

"Maybe they had a secret code," said Bob. "Like the book code Li Chang used to hide his message about the hidden gold." He said this not because he really believed it, but to cheer Freya up.

It worked, because she suddenly looked at him, her eyes shining. "If you wanted to come to our house in Palisade Point, I could translate the letters into English out loud. Really. All of you are welcome. You could come tomorrow, if you wanted," she said.

"We can't come tomorrow," Pete said. "Tomorrow we've got an appointment to see Per Jorgensen, the Danish actor who donated the painting to the Center."

"Per Jorgensen!" said Leif. "I know his work very well. Up until *The Seventh Messenger* he was mostly known in Scandinavia, not in America. But Magnus and I grew up watching his movies. You will actually meet him tomorrow?"

"We've been invited to his house," Pete said. "And since we haven't had time to call Worthington to see if he can take us, maybe you could drive us in the Ford Flex. If Aunt Mathilda says it's O.K., of course."

"I bet she would," said Jupiter. "You know how star struck she was after she met Sir Iain Anthony. She didn't stop talking about it for days!"

Bob noticed that once again the conversation had moved away from something Freya had contributed, so he was glad when Jupiter added, to Freya, "But even if we can't come tomorrow, we should certainly come to your house soon. I'd like to see the Olsen painting your parents own, and it's quite possible that the letters will give us information we couldn't get otherwise. I don't know if Kalberg mentioned the paintings to your grandfather, but I would guess that he wrote about his assignment with the German officer – if not during the war, then after it."

Freya looked pleased that her invitation had been accepted, and Bob could tell that Leif and Magnus were also pleased. Obviously, Bob understood, their real task at the Salvage

Yard was not to help Freya make a loom but to help her get out of her online world, and into the real one, and this was a step in the right direction. He was rooting for her.

"Great!" Bob said. "We'll find a time soon when we can all go to your house."

"And you'll come too?" Freya said, looking at Mallory.

Bob could see Mallory was touched.

"Sure," she said. "Thank you."

Bob was reminded again of why he liked Mallory so much. It looked like she and Freya would get along after all, Bob thought, as they all said goodbye, and he and Mallory and Jupe and Pete headed out and closed the door behind them.

"Well, maybe that's enough investigating for now," Bob said. "My stomach's growling. Do you guys want to come to my house for lunch? We have plenty of stuff for sandwiches."

"And I'll take a double helping of it all!" Pete said.

Bob thought of saying that "taking a double helping" was supposed to be a metaphor for someone's enthusiastic agreement, not a literal description of someone actually getting a double helping at lunch – but when Pete added, "It's great to have a Virgo organizing

things! Bob's the foundation of the firm!" – he
didn't.

He was flattered by Pete's description,
but secretly he'd always found the characteris-
tics of a Virgo a bit – well – unexciting. Virgos
were dutiful and precise and even-tempered
and methodical. Maybe that was why he'd always been so glad to be part of the always-sur-
prising and frequently-exciting Three Investigators!

7

An Enlightening Visit

That night, Pete tossed and turned, trying to get to sleep. He kept remembering the Haldorssons' story about the three men who had joined the Norwegian Resistance and then become friends with a German officer they had previously thought of as an enemy. It seemed to Pete quite significant, somehow, that there were three of them.

At dinner, he'd gotten his father talking about the work he'd done on *The Seventh Messenger*, and now Pete's thoughts turned to the movie. When his father had taken him to see it, Pete had been electrified by Per Jorgensen – his fierceness with a heavy double-bladed sword, his skill with horses, the hooded look in his eye when he sent his falcon out to hunt. And now he was going to actually meet him!

Pete woke later than he'd expected the next morning, and after he showered and dressed, he rode his bike to the Salvage Yard – racing faster than he thought he ever had before. He got there flustered and hot and sweaty, and the first thing he did was ask Bob,

133

"Is my face bright red?"

"Yes," Bob said. "You look like you overdid it. Drink some water."

"I was late!" Pete said. He fanned himself with his hand. His stomach felt jumpy and he couldn't keep still. When he was like this, his friends said he was as skittery as a jackrabbit. He tucked in his shirt and tried to cool down.

A little while later, with the window open for air, he sat in the back of the Flex, Bob beside him, Jupiter at the other window, with Mallory riding in the front seat. Just as Jupiter had predicted, Aunt Mathilda had given Leif permission to drive them, and they were on their way to Per Jorgensen's house on the coast. As they drove, Leif was talking intensely about one of Per Jorgensen's Danish movies, *Tempest Island* – a movie Pete hadn't seen.

Oddly enough, it was a World War Two drama, and part of it took place on a small island off the coast of Denmark. Per Jorgensen played a Danish resistance fighter watching the sea for German U-boats. Listening to Leif talking, Pete stared out the window at the Pacific as they rode south on Highway One. The ocean glittered brilliantly, and below them a fringe of surf marked where the water met the land. As far as he could see, there were no U-boats out there.

"He speaks Norwegian, too," Leif was saying. "But not in *Tempest Island*."

"Does he catch any Nazis?" Pete asked.

"No, but he fights some!" Leif said.

As the Flex came around a slow curve, Pete saw, on the ocean side of the road, a hand-carved wooden totem pole with a raven with outspread wings on the top. "There it is!" Pete said, pointing.

"Yes!" Leif said. "Here we are!" He slowed the Flex and turned down a dirt drive-way. Per Jorgensen had said they'd know they'd found his house by the totem pole. All of them – but Pete in particular – had been on the lookout. The driveway was rutted from last winter's rains and Leif steered carefully from side to side, avoiding the low spots as best he could. Not far ahead, Pete could see what looked like a classic one-story California beach cottage perched on the steep hillside, with a footpath descending to the sea. The cottage was small, sheathed in gray weathered shingles, with a low-slope roof and a deck on stilts facing west – where the Pacific went on and on. It didn't look like a movie star's house, but Pete was wild about it.

Leif pulled up next to a weathered Jeep,

and as the five of them got out of the car, Pete looked up to see Per Jorgensen come out to meet them, accompanied by a regal black and tan German shepherd who stayed close to his side. She was sleek and slim.

Per Jorgensen looked − well, Pete thought − like Per Jorgensen! He was tall and slender and rugged-looking, with broad shoulders and narrow hips. His hair was dark with streaks of blond and it looked like Jorgensen had just toweled it after taking a shower. His intense gray eyes, high cheekbones, and square stubbled chin made him seem both forbidding and friendly at the same time. He bristled with vitality.

Jorgensen turned to the Shepherd. "Brigitte," he said, "sit."

The dog sat immediately and looked calm and alert.

Swallowing hard, Pete walked up to him. "Mr. Jorgensen!" he said. "I'm Pete Crenshaw. You know my father Martín."

"I certainly do," Per Jorgensen said, shaking Pete's hand. "How is he?"

"Really good, thank you!" Pete said. "And thanks for agreeing to see us."

By this time the others had crowded around, and Pete introduced his friends one by one. Jorgensen shook everyone's hand, smiling, as though he were greeting a bunch of old friends. Leif, who Pete thought of as a natural talker, seemed a little bit tongue-tied.

"Jer er glad o møte deg," he stammered.

Jorgensen laughed in surprise. "And I am glad to meet you too!" he said. "Are you Norwegian?"

"Yes," Leif said. "I'm a big fan."

"This is Brigitte," Jorgensen said. He gestured to the Shepherd. "She's very friendly – and also very brave. Brigitte, say hello." Pete laughed as Brigitte raised her paw and offered it to Leif, and then to anyone who wanted to shake it. Pete certainly did. The dog had a thick luxurious coat, and her eyes shone with intelligence.

"Come in, come in," Jorgensen said, as he ushered them toward the door.

The inside of Per Jorgensen's house was as unpretentious as the outside. The main room had comfortable chairs and a sofa, all positioned so that you couldn't help but look out the wall of windows overlooking the ocean. On the other walls were simple colorful prints of sea birds. Pete was happy to see that Per Jorgensen collected wooden carvings. He saw a number of carved seals and a starfish so detailed it looked almost real.

"These are great!" he said, turning to Jorgensen.

"Thank you," Per Jorgensen said. "They keep me busy."

"You carved these?" Pete asked.

"Yes," the actor said. "When I'm feeling moody, I walk on the beach and pick up scraps of wood I find. Usually they suggest some creature to me."

"Did you do the totem pole too?" Pete asked, as it suddenly dawned on him that this was a possibility. He remembered the carved whale that Rafael Solares had given The Three Investigators as a memento of their last adventure. "It must be cool to do art like that!" he added. "I don't think I have the talent."

"What do you mean?" Bob asked, quite seriously. "It was Pete who thought up a really cool logo for our firm!" he explained. "It's a chimera – a mythical figure that Pete re-imagined for the three of us. In it, Jupiter is a golden eagle, I'm a bobcat, and Pete is a big mountain sheep with curling horns. Very intimidating!" Pete started to blush.

"One for all and all for one!" Per Jorgensen said. He turned to Pete. "When it comes to carving wood, I think you might find it very restful. Mostly it's about being careful and patient," he said.

"That lets me out," Pete said.

Pete was happy to find that there were other people in the world who weren't snobs about art that actually looked like what it was supposed to represent. With all the talk about fancy modern art that had been swirling around the last few days, Pete had felt a little out of it. But Per Jorgensen, of all people, seemed to like what *he* liked – plain simple carvings and sculptures and paintings.

Jupiter had also been looking at the objects displayed in Jorgensen's house, and now he walked over to a shelf where two leather falconer's gauntlets had been laid out, side by side. Pete followed him over and when Jupiter said, about the one on the right, "This is very fine workmanship," Pete added "I like the little tassel! And the circular emblem on the big part of the glove!"

Jorgensen nodded. "That particular gauntlet was made for me for my role in *The Seventh Messenger*. The costume designer was kind enough to give it to me as a memento of the film."

"I love mementos!" Pete said. "Jupe and Bob and I have started to collect them after our cases. We've got five of them displayed in Headquarters already!"

Per Jorgensen smiled at his enthusiasm. "Your father told me that you guys are detectives, and that you want to help the Center For Falconry and Fencing recover the painting I gave them. How are you connected to the Center?"

"Jupiter is taking lessons there. He's thinking of fencing in high school," Pete said.

"We'll have to take up foils," Per Jorgensen said, nodding encouragingly at Jupiter. "Though I parried with heavier blades."

"And I'm just starting," Jupiter said. "I went for my first lesson, and when I went back for my second, I discovered that the painting you gave the Center had been stolen the night before."

Jupiter took out his wallet, extracted one of the Three Investigators' business cards, and handed it to Per Jorgensen. The card read:

THE THREE INVESTIGATORS
"We Investigate Anything"
???
First Investigator – Jupiter Jones
Second Investigator – Pete Crenshaw
Records and Research – Bob Andrews

At the bottom was the number of the landline in Headquarters, the number of Bob's cell-phone, and the website address of their firm.

That did it! Pete thought. This was now officially a case!

Jorgensen studied the card, then looked questioningly at Mallory.

"Mallory is our friend," Bob said quickly. "We met her just a few months ago, when she moved here from Scotland. But she's helped us out in almost every case we've had this summer."

"Well," Mallory said. "I've tried."

"She's been invaluable at several junctures," Jupiter said.

Mallory looked pleased, but as Pete glanced back at Per Jorgensen, an expression crossed his face that was hard for Pete to read.

"The Three Investigators," he said. "Why does that ring a bell?"

He thought for a moment, and then looked relieved. "Why, of course!" he said. "You're the boys who helped dispel those vicious rumors about my friend Sir Iain Anthony!"

"You know Sir Iain?" Pete asked.

"Yes," Per Jorgensen said. "I've done a

little stage work, and Sir Iain is an old friend. The article I read was quite clear that you saved his reputation and his position at the summer theater in Rocky Beach."

"That's where we live," Bob said. "A friend of ours was playing Juliet in a production there, which is how we got involved."

"Do you know Daman Duwalia?" Pete asked.

"That young whippersnapper?" Per Jorgensen said. "Of course! But let's get down to business. You didn't come here to talk about the movies."

That was true, Pete thought – though he'd wouldn't have minded talking about them just a little bit longer.

"Thanks for your business card," Per Jorgensen said. "I hope you'll be as successful with your search for the stolen painting as you were with what you did for Sir Iain."

He removed his wallet, inserted their card, then pulled out his own.

"You should call me if you need my help," he said, as he handed the card to Pete. Pete looked at it with astonishment, then passed it to Bob to keep.

"Bob's Records and Research," he explained. "And he's the one who always has his cellphone."

"I haven't been out for my morning walk yet. Would you like to wander down to the ocean so we can talk there?" Jorgensen said.

The house had been built into the hillside, and below them, through the giant windows, Pete saw the scarf of white sand where the waves came in, and then the ocean for as far as he could see. He looked at Jupiter and Bob, who seemed a little uncertain, but Mallory and Leif were ready, and in no time at all, they were all scrambling down the dirt path that led to the sea – Brigitte leading the way.

The wind off the water was bracing and smelled of sun and salt. When they got down to the small sandy beach, they started walking south. Pete found himself next to Jorgensen and Brigitte.

"You said Brigitte was brave?" Pete said.

Jorgensen looked down at her proudly. "When she and I were walking in a part of Los Angeles I was unfamiliar with one evening, she saved me from a mugging. She bit the mugger – though she clearly knew that he might hurt her. That's what courage is – being brave when you know you could be hurt, or when you're truly frightened."

"Pete knows that already," Bob said.

"He should have been a lion in our chimera."

Pete blushed a second time.

Per Jorgensen seemed not to notice as he looked from Brigitte to the waves, then suggested that they all settle down on the sand in front of some weathered rocks. Once they were seated, he went on. "But maybe lions *aren't* brave! With the exception of human beings, any predator at the top of its food chain isn't likely to be frightened by anything. Certainly falcons aren't. I learned that when I was studying at the Center."

"How long did you study there?" Jupiter asked, sitting forward and clasping his hands around his knees.

"Let's see," Per Jorgensen said. The sun bounced off the water and bathed his face in a golden light. "When they offered me the role in *The Seventh Messenger* – "

"Fantastic movie!" Pete said.

Jorgensen smiled. "I had done some sword work before, but I knew nothing about falconry. When I studied it, I learned that falcons aren't afraid of anything – though human beings are! Still, in a way, a falconer is like an artist. Or to put it another way, all true artists have to be falconers. Both artists and falconers clearly see the nature of life. Beautiful as it is, nothing will ever make it perfect, because it always ends in death, and there's a lot of pain along the way. That's always an artist's truest truth."

Whoa! thought Pete. That was pretty heavy. But while he didn't understand all of it, exactly, he was glad that Per Jorgensen had felt free to say it to the four of them. And after all, it *had* been art that had brought them to his house today.

"But to get back to your question," Jorgensen continued. "Though I'd been in some historical films before, the medieval era was new to me. The people at the Center couldn't have been nicer or more knowledgeable, and I worked with them for over four months.

"I would have been grateful anyway, but when I was nominated for the Oscar, I wanted to do something special to thank them. I was walking down Wilshire Boulevard one day about five months ago, and I stopped in front of this art gallery window where this painting of a medieval falconer was displayed. I knew right away it was the perfect gift."

"I can see why," Jupiter said.

"So I brought the painting home," Per Jorgensen said, "and began planning a bequest that would accompany it. Then, about a month ago – and just a week before I was going to present the painting to the Center – the strangest thing happened. I got a letter from a lawyer working at a famous Los Angeles firm, offering to buy the painting."

Yikes! Pete thought. That *was* odd.

"Why did the lawyer want the painting?" Bob asked.

"He didn't," Jorgensen said. "He was writing on behalf of a client, who wished to remain anonymous. The client was offering many times what I had paid for the painting."

"But you told the lawyer no," Jupiter said.

"I did," Per Jorgensen said. "I told him it was intended as a gift for the Center for Falconry and Fencing and was not for sale. I also told him I was sure that the Center wouldn't sell it to him either."

"Uh oh," Pete said. "So the lawyer's client knew where the painting was going to wind up."

"Yes," Per Jorgensen said. "I wish now I hadn't told him."

"So it's logical to assume," Jupiter said, "that when the client couldn't get his hands on the painting by buying it from you that he took the next and quite unusual step of stealing it.

Have you told this to the police?"

"No," Per Jorgensen said. "They asked me only a few rudimentary questions. They wanted to know why I had given the painting to the Center, and where I had bought it."

Out over the water, in the blue California air, a tern swooped, catching Pete's eye. He thought, and not for the first time, how graceful they were, and how much he wished he could fly.

"What's that?" Leif suddenly said, pointing.

Everyone turned to look out to sea.

"What do you think you saw?" Per Jorgensen said. "Sometimes seals come into this cove and sun themselves on the beach."

Leif started laughing. "No," he said. "I was telling all of them about your movie *Tempest Island* earlier, and I thought I just saw a U-boat surfacing! My imagination got the better of me."

"There's a rock out in the water," Per Jorgensen said. "Sometimes it's hidden by the tide, and sometimes it's just barely visible. It looks a little like a conning tower."

Jupiter cleared his throat. "If I may ask," he said, "we'd be interested to know where you bought the painting."

"Certainly," Per Jorgensen said. "As I mentioned before, I saw it in the window of a gallery on Wilshire Boulevard. It's named after the owner and manager of the gallery — Matthias Mueller Limited."

"Matthias Mueller!" Pete exclaimed. "That's the second big coincidence in this case!"

"The third, really," Bob said. "If you count Jupiter meeting Günther Böhm, and then Matthias Mueller telling us about him at Lyle and Cornelius's party."

Per Jorgensen looked at Bob questioningly. "You know Matthias Mueller?"

"We don't actually know him," Jupiter told him, "but we met him the other night at a fund-raising party in Sherman Oaks."

"A fund-raising party?" Per Jorgensen asked, smiling broadly. "I get invited to those all the time, but I wouldn't think that you would!"

"It's a long story," said Jupiter. "But I'd appreciate knowing more about your own meeting with Matthias Mueller."

"A very nice man," Per Jorgensen said. "He told me that he'd obtained a number of paintings similar to the one I bought at an auction house in Germany."

"Did he say how many?" Bob asked, excited.

"Not exactly," Per Jorgensen said. "But he did mention that they all featured a medieval falconer. For obvious reasons he didn't have them all on display at the same time, but from the description he gave me, they were very much alike."

Jupiter was always quite restrained, so Pete was rather surprised when he jumped to his feet and began pacing back and forth on the sand. Brigitte had been lying next to Per Jorgensen, but Jupiter's sudden movement made her get up and bark.

"Brigitte," Per Jorgensen said. "It's all right." Brigitte settled herself again, and Jorgensen looked at Jupiter, puzzled.

"He gets like this when he's excited," Pete said helpfully. "Though he's normally not this excited."

"I must confess," Jupiter said, looking at Pete and nodding, "that I wasn't sure what we might learn from our visit with you, Mr. Jorgensen. But you have given us more important information than I could have wished for."

Now everyone got to their feet and began walking back up the beach. Pete looked at Jupiter, whose eyes were gleaming. He was also pinching his lower lip. Pete could see that Jupiter had put two and two together, and expectantly, he waited for four.

"We learned the other night," Jupiter said, "that Mr. Mueller had a number of paintings for sale, quite similar to one another, and it's now obvious that the painting you bought, Mr. Jorgensen, was one of them. And you just said that Mr. Mueller bought them at an auction house in Berlin a year and a half ago."

"That's what I learned from Mueller," Per Jorgensen said.

"We also know that a German artist named Günther Böhm came into Mr. Mueller's gallery and wanted to buy one of the paintings," Jupiter went on. "But Mr. Mueller disliked Böhm and refused to sell it to him. He took it home instead."

"If Günther Böhm wanted to buy one painting of a medieval falconer —" Bob said.

"Then maybe he's the one who was trying to buy your painting, Mr. Jorgensen," Pete said.

"And when he found he couldn't," Bob said, "maybe he simply stole it. Or had it stolen."

"I think the next thing we need to do," Jupiter said, "is take Mr. Mueller up on his invitation to visit him at his gallery."

Gee whiz! Pete thought. It was amazing how The Three Investigators' cases came together. He looked at his friends. Jupiter, Bob, and Mallory all looked elated. The chase was on!

"But," Pete said. "Wait a minute. Why in the world would this Günther Böhm want so many different paintings of falconers?"

"That," Jupiter said, "is a very good question!"

Per Jorgensen reached over and picked up a piece of driftwood mottled blond and black. He stared at it for a minute and then handed it to Pete.

"If you look carefully, my friend," he said, "you'll find a tern – or maybe a falcon – wanting to be carved."

Pete stared at the piece of wood and could almost see what Per Jorgensen had suggested. He turned the driftwood over, then thrust it into his pocket.

"Gee, thanks!" he said. "And thanks for the tip about Matthias Mueller! It was very enlightening!"

8

Jupiter Jumps To A Few Conclusions

On the way back up the path to Per Jorgensen's cottage, Jupiter found himself a little winded. It was to be expected, he thought; after all, the hillside was unusually steep. Still, he didn't see Mallory or Pete or Bob huffing and puffing, and he made a mental note to get a bit more in shape. He wanted to fence well, and fitness and stamina would have to be part of the training regimen.

Jupiter and the others stood by the Flex and the Jeep as everyone thanked Per Jorgensen for his time and hospitality. Jupiter was the last to shake Mr. Jorgensen's hand, and he did so with gratitude and pleasure. Jupiter was always impressed by people like Jorgensen – blessed by nature with extraordinary looks, or by hard work and luck with extraordinary fame, who nonetheless seemed unimpressed with themselves. Per Jorgensen had been friendly and affable and without pretense, and he had been a very great help.

And not just with the information he had given about Matthias Mueller's gallery, Jupiter thought, but also with what he had said about artists and falconry. Although Jupiter wasn't sure just why Jorgensen's comments had struck a chord with him, he intended to think about it further, as soon as he had a chance to do so. In the meantime, everyone was saying good-bye.

"Now let me know how your investigation progresses!" Jorgensen said to Jupiter. "I'd very much like to see that painting returned to the Center, so perhaps I can help. And good luck with that piece of wood, Pete!"

"Thanks," Pete said bashfully, and then they all clambered back into the Flex and drove off waving. When they got to the head of the driveway and Highway One, Jupiter asked Leif to turn right, toward Los Angeles.

"Right?" Leif said. "I don't think so. Don't you want to go back to the Salvage Yard?"

"No," Jupiter said. "Strike while the iron is hot! I was hoping you'd drive us into Santa Monica, so we can pay a visit to Matthias Mueller's art gallery."

Leif paused, looking doubtful. "I don't know, Jupiter," he said. "Your aunt expects me back soon, and Magnus and I were late just the other day."

Leif was a very good and conscientious worker, and Jupiter knew he didn't like being away from his job for longer than necessary.

"You can blame it on me," he said. "Aunt Mathilda will forgive me with my birthday coming up, and beside, you've got a real connection to this case, Leif. Your parents own a painting a lot like the one Per Jorgensen bought. The mystery is yours as well."

"That's true!" Leif said. "All right. Let's go! But I think we should call your aunt when we get to the gallery."

Jupiter was glad that Leif had been easy to convince, because the visit with Per Jorgensen had reaped unexpected results, and Jupiter's mind was whirring. He felt excited and fully alive; everything looked just a bit brighter. When he felt like this, he had learned it was always best to act. Mental acuity was not to be wasted!

Wilshire Boulevard ran from Santa Monica to downtown Los Angeles, and Jupiter was glad that Mr. Mueller's gallery was at the Santa Monica end. He disliked the towering buildings and urban congestion of downtown L.A., with its hordes of pedestrians and its flaunted wealth. Even Santa Monica was considerably more urban than he liked. It took a little while, but they finally found Matthias Mueller Limited, which occupied the street level of a four-story building.

The front windows held several paintings set up on easels with pinpoint spotlights illuminating them, even in the middle of the day. This was how Per Jorgensen had first come across the painting he'd bought, Jupiter thought. The ones on display today were all geometric abstracts – brightly colored boxes and triangles and lines, which looked as though they'd been painted by the same artist.

Leif stayed with the car, but the others followed Jupiter as he opened the door with its gilt letters and stepped through into the cool dim interior. Jupiter could see Matthias Mueller in the back of the shop, talking to a customer, but Werner Mueller and Dika Horváth both saw the small crowd enter and hurried to greet them.

"Welcome!" Werner said. "I was afraid I might not see you again before I went back to Germany."

"Can we help you find a painting?" Dika asked. "I wouldn't have thought you were rich enough to afford one, but one can always hope! I get a commission on every painting that I sell."

This was a joke, Jupiter understood — and yet not quite a joke, somehow. With his mind already whirring from the meeting with Per Jorgensen, he was in the mood to file anything out of the ordinary in a special section of his brain, and he did that now with Dika's comment about money.

"So why *have* you come today?" Werner said. "I have a suspicion this is not merely a social call."

"You're correct," Jupiter said, smiling. "We have some questions we need to ask your uncle. But for now, I can ask *you* one. The other night at the party, you were there when your uncle told us a story about an obnoxious man he wouldn't sell a painting to — and you were still there when Günther Böhm, the man himself, showed up. I'm sure you remember."

"Of course," Werner said. "I'm afraid I may never forget!"

"Was the painting he wanted to buy of a man dressed as a medieval falconer holding a falcon?" Jupiter asked.

Werner looked thunderstruck. "Why, yes," he said. "The painting Böhm wanted *was* of a falconer and is now in my uncle's house. But as he told you the other night, there were others very much like it — though different in

156

size and shape."

Jupiter could see that Dika Horváth seemed unusually interested in this conversation. He wondered if she'd also been in the shop the day that Günther Böhm had been there.

"Did you meet Günther Böhm, too?" he asked her.

Dika wrinkled her brow and put her hands on her hips, then shook her head slowly.

"You know, I really can't be certain. I think I may have seen him when I was dealing with another customer. But I'm pretty sure I never talked to him myself."

To Jupiter, there was something about the way she said this that seemed less than perfectly sincere, so he wasn't surprised when Werner said, "I think you did, Dika. In fact, I thought I saw you showing him your mini-trampoline. You remember? You brought it in that day and stuck it in a corner. You had a gig that evening at a children's party in Santa Monica."

"Was it *that* day?" Dika asked in apparent surprise. "Yes, now that you mention it, I think you may be right."

"Are you a gymnast?" Jupiter asked, as casually as he could.

"I am," Dika said. "I came to California with a Romanian circus, but when they were finished with their tour here, they moved on to New York. I had a one-year work visa, so I decided to stay in California to perform with a dance troupe that offered me a job. But they were terrible! Soon we had no bookings and everyone went their separate ways. I had no idea what to do, but I didn't want to go back to Romania before I had to. Mr. Mueller had just put up a 'Help Wanted' sign when I walked by the door, so I was very lucky."

She smiled a big, disarming smile. "I'm making extra money by performing at children's parties."

Just then, Matthias Mueller said goodbye to the customer he'd been talking to and walked toward them, obviously pleased to see them.

"Hallo, hallo!" he called. "Guten tag! What brings all of you here today?"

To Dika, he added, "Could you attend to that customer while I talk to the boys?" She nodded and left.

Jupiter said, "We've just come from visiting the Danish actor Per Jorgensen, who told us that he recently bought a painting from your shop."

"He *did* buy a painting from me," Matthias Mueller said. "It was before Dika started to work here, and before Werner arrived for the summer. Five months ago now, I think."

"I'm glad to get that confirmed," Jupiter said. "As you know, Pete, Bob, and I have an investigative firm, and we're investigating the theft of that painting – which Per Jorgensen gave to the Center for Falconry and Fencing."

"The painting he bought here was stolen?" Matthias Mueller asked in alarm.

"Yes," said Jupiter. "In the night, just a few days ago. And yesterday morning we discovered that ten paintings by the Norwegian artist Aksel Olsen were sold by an auction house in Berlin a year and a half ago. Since Per Jorgensen told us that he bought his at your gallery, we have deduced that, when you told us at the fund-raiser about a group of paintings you bought at an auction house in Germany, you were referring to the Aksel Olsen paintings."

"A very accurate deduction!" Matthias Mueller said. "The painting I told you about the other night – the one I wouldn't sell to the obnoxious artist Günther Böhm is also one of those ten."

"What do you know about the history of the paintings? Can you tell us why you bought them?" Jupiter asked.

"Of course," Mueller said. "Every year I go back to Germany on business, and I make the rounds of the various auction houses. I have to be very careful – thinking about what my clientele back here might like. I knew almost nothing about the Olsen paintings, and the catalogue was very skimpy on details. But I was drawn to them, somehow. I felt they were more than they at first appeared. And I was right, because I have managed to sell every single one of them – except the one I kept."

"Do you know who put them up for sale?" Jupiter asked. "Who the previous owner was?"

"Hartung & Hartung – the auction house in Berlin – is renowned for its discretion. It offers absolute anonymity to the person who is putting the work up for sale. And this was an auction of minor work, so provenance was not so important as at other auctions I have been to."

"Provenance," Jupiter said. "Could you explain that term?"

"Surely," Mueller said. "Provenance refers to the history of a piece of art – who created it, when and where, who owned it, who owned it next, and so forth. We use it to establish the authenticity and sometimes the quality of the piece."

"I see," Jupiter said.

"This particular auction house," Mueller said, "has an excellent reputation – unlike a number of others, which might be called notorious. As you know, many works of art were stolen during the Second World War. In many cases, descendants of the owners have been trying for years to reclaim the art that was stolen. Some of it, of course, was extremely valuable – in the millions of dollars."

"Yes," Bob said, intently. "We were reading about that. About how the Nazis labeled modern art 'degenerate' and seized it – but were then not above selling it to others and making a profit from it. Or keeping it, to enjoy in secret."

"Sadly, that is exactly right," Mueller said. "In Germany in particular, the theft and destruction of art was a monumental scandal and tragedy."

"But what about the history of the Aksel Olsen paintings?" Jupiter asked.

"In this case, the provenance is a bit disordered," Mueller said. "It's known that Aksel

Olsen painted the ten paintings in Oslo – not long before he was shot by the Nazis. But I don't know who first owned them, or who put them up for sale. Still, I trust Hartung & Hartung not to sell anything they have reason to be suspicious about."

"Do you have any idea why an artist would paint essentially the same painting over and over again?" Mallory asked suddenly. "It seems like a strange thing to do."

"It is quite unusual," Mueller conceded. "But sometimes painters get so interested in one thing that they cannot help repeating themselves in one way or another. They may paint for a year or more in a particular style and then never repeat it. But I do take your point. What Olsen did is, in my experience, unique."

"But he was clearly onto something!" Bob said, "If you managed to sell all ten of the paintings."

"Nine," Mueller said. "I have the one at home, hanging on my wall."

"That reminds me," Jupiter said. "Would you be willing to give us a list of the people who bought the Olsen paintings? We know about Per Jorgensen, of course. But could you give us the names and addresses of the other eight?"

"It's a bit irregular to give out the names of customers," Mr. Mueller said, "but since you are detectives, trying to find a stolen painting, I think I can bend the rules. Come with me."

Jupiter and the others followed Mr. Mueller to the back of the gallery where he had a small office walled off from the rest of the shop. Mueller took the glasses he had perched on top of his head and put them on. Then, with a few swift keystrokes on his computer, he pulled up a list of paintings, hit PRINT, and soon a sheet of paper came out of Mr. Mueller's printer.

"There you are," he said, giving the paper to Jupiter.

Jupiter saw there were nine paintings listed in one column as Aksel Olsen # 1, Aksel Olsen # 2, and so forth, the names and addresses of the buyers in subsequent columns, and finally the amount that had been paid.

"Your painting isn't listed here," Jupiter said.

"No!" Mr. Mueller said. "Because I didn't sell it to myself!"

"I understand," Jupiter said. He saw that the owners of the paintings were scattered all over southern California. It might take some real work to track them down.

"Well, thank you very much, Mr. Mueller," he said. He looked to the front of the shop where Dika was still talking to the customer Matthias Mueller had asked her to attend to. He hoped he could talk to her again before he left.

"Have you heard from Lyle and Cornelius?" Mallory suddenly asked Mr. Mueller. "Is any progress being made on saving the Voronin murals?"

"No one has touched them yet," Mr. Mueller said, "and no one will if Lyle Smith has anything to say about it. The committee he's formed − and I'm happy to say that I'm on it! − has a special petition for high school teachers, and we're trying to get as many signatures as possible. Who better to stand up for the murals than teachers? Do you know any high school teachers you could give the petition to?" he said to the group.

"We haven't started high school quite yet," Bob said. "But it won't be long now."

"That's right!" Pete said. "In less than two weeks!"

"We're particularly interested in finding people who taught at the high school where the murals were painted, and of course that goes back a long time now − nearly eighty years," Mr. Mueller said. "Though, really, we're happy to get the signatures of *any* teachers!"

"We do know two teachers," Bob said. "I don't know if either of them ever taught at the high school where the murals are. I'm pretty sure one of them spent his whole career up in Rocky Beach. But the other teacher might have. We'd have to ask. They're both retired."

"Do you mean Wally Tate and Isabella Chang?" Mallory asked.

"Yes," Bob said. "You've met Wally, but you haven't met Isabella yet. I'm sure you'd like her a lot. I can't imagine anyone not liking her."

"She's great!" Pete said.

"Maybe you and I can go visit them and ask them to sign the petition tomorrow," Bob said to Mallory.

"That's a good plan," Jupiter said. "Pete and I will try to track down the people on this list" − he waved the printout with the names of the buyers of the Aksel Olsen paintings − "and you two can go to Isabella Chang's house, then join us in the Salvage Yard."

"If you're going tomorrow," Mr. Mueller said, "then let me give you copies of the petition." From a folder on his desk he drew out a number of sheets of paper.

"This first packet," he said, "gives the history of the murals, as well as images of them. Then there's the history of the controversy and some copies of recent newspaper articles about the school board's decision. The petition is here."

He handed Bob another sheet.

"As you can see, there's a place for the teachers to print and sign their names and addresses, and a place for them to write any comments they might have about the situation," he added.

"Thanks!" Bob said. "I'm sure Wally and Isabella will sign. In fact, knowing the two of them, they might form their own committee!"

Bob took the papers and tucked them carefully away in the zipped portfolio he almost always carried with him.

"Goodbye, then," Jupiter said. "I'm sure we'll be seeing more of you."

"I hope so," Werner said. "Let me walk you to the door."

"Lovely to see you all," Mr. Mueller said. "Enjoy the rest of your afternoon."

Jupiter was thinking hard on the way

out. He held the paper in one hand, while with the other he pinched his lower lip. Of course, since they had the owners' addresses, they could drive up to their houses, knock on their doors, and ask about the paintings. But there had to be a quicker way. The telephone seemed like a good idea, although getting reverse phone numbers when you knew someone's address wasn't as easy as it had once been.

"Wow!" Pete said, staring up at the wall as they passed. "Mr. Mueller has all kinds of art for sale!"

He was staring at what looked to Jupiter like a painting of a zebra with its head where its hindquarters should be, but after glancing at it for a moment, Jupiter saw that Dika had said goodbye to the customer she'd been talking to, and he paused to let her catch up to them.

Unfortunately, before Jupiter could come up with a plan to question her further, the door to the shop opened and two middle-aged women carrying very large handbags walked in. They stopped and looked around as if they didn't quite know what to do next.

"Excuse me," Dika said. "I've worked here long enough to know those women might actually buy something, even though they don't know much about art. And commissions have a way of adding up!"

Werner laughed, and Dika moved away again, so after saying goodbye to Werner, Jupiter and the others walked out into the glare of a California summer afternoon.

It was hot in the city – a lot hotter than it was in Rocky Beach – and Jupiter looked forward to getting home. The sun bounced off the asphalt street and the concrete sidewalk and the glass storefronts; the noise of automobile engines and construction machinery created a steady irritating drone in the background.

As the four of them greeted Leif and climbed into the Flex, Leif insisted that Bob call Jupiter's aunt right away, while Jupiter settled back into his seat to think. This case had built a little slowly, he thought, and it might never become the most gripping case they'd ever had, but as the pieces started to come together, he thought they were actually quite interesting. Although Jupiter had no real reason to suspect that Dika Horváth was dishonest, the fact that she was a gymnast seemed rather suspicious, under the circumstances.

In fact, although he knew he might be jumping the gun on this, Jupiter couldn't help but wonder if Dika Horváth and Günther Böhm were in cahoots.

Could Günther Böhm have hired Dika Horváth to steal the falcon painting from the Center, after Böhm tried to buy it from Per Jorgensen, and Jorgensen refused to sell it?

More than that, could Dika Horváth have given Günther Böhm the list of clients to whom Matthias Mueller had sold the paintings? By printing them off from Mueller's computer, just as Mueller himself had? She had made it clear that she liked (or needed) money – which Günther Böhm apparently had a lot of.

If she had provided Böhm with that list of buyers at the beginning of the summer, when she had just started to work at Matthias Mueller's shop, then she might have considered herself already involved in Günther Böhm's scheme when he asked her to take her involvement a step further.

But what *was* his scheme, exactly? Why had he tried to buy one of these Aksel Olsens and then – presumably – stolen another one? Or hired a Romanian gymnast to steal it for him?

There were too many questions and not enough answers. Jupiter hoped that when he and Pete started to track down the people on Matthias Mueller's list, what he already suspected would be confirmed – that Günther Böhm was trying to get his hands on all of the Aksel Olsen paintings.

One thing was certain: Although Günther Böhm might call himself an artist, and might even have managed to convince other people that he *was* one, from the moment Jupiter met him, it had been obvious that the man was nothing but a phony.

In fact, when Jupiter thought back on what Per Jorgensen had said about a true artist clearly seeing that nothing would ever make human life perfect – because pain and suffering were a fundamental part of existence – he couldn't help but think that Günther Böhm might be the exact *opposite* of a true artist, in every way that really mattered.

A sort of counterfeit artist, really – and one who shouldn't be allowed near the work of anyone else. It was a pity that the paintings his father and grandfather had collected before and after the Second World War were being treated so disrespectfully by their puffed-up and peculiar adoptee, Jupiter thought.

Even so, he couldn't shake the feeling that he was missing something important, and as he looked at Mallory, sitting in the seat in front of him, he half wished he hadn't agreed that she and Bob should spend the first part of the following morning at Isabella Chang's house. While Pete was a fabulous Second, and as brave as a lion, he wasn't as good as Bob and Mallory at being a sounding board for Jupiter's own still-unformed thoughts.

9

Mallory Misses A Clue

That evening, as Mallory got ready for bed in her bedroom at the Wessex House, she found herself thinking pretty much the same thing — although, in her case, it was her mother, not Pete, who was less than perceptive about Mallory's not-yet-formed-or-realized thoughts.

At dinner, the two of them had been talking about the Voronin murals, and when Mallory had told her mother her plans for the following morning, as well as what had been happening, her mother had seemed to be off in her own world.

"You know Per Jorgensen, the actor, right?" Mallory had said.

Her mother had looked at her doubtfully. "His name's familiar," she said.

"Then I guess you don't," Mallory said. "I've never seen him in a movie, but I could tell how good he must be. Plus, the things he said about falconry and falconers were fascinating."

"What did he say?" her mother asked.

"That falcons aren't afraid of anything — though human beings are! That life isn't kind, and that both falconers and artists have to see that nothing will ever make it perfect, because it always ends in death or loss. I'm not talking about Daddy, just everyone," Mallory added.

To her dismay, her mother had started crying. Now, as Mallory climbed into bed and pulled the covers up, she lay for awhile, thinking in the darkness. While she certainly couldn't blame her mother for crying, she sometimes got tired of people trying to pretend that life on earth could be a perfect paradise.

It would never be a perfect paradise, Mallory thought, and one of the reasons she sometimes had trouble making friends was that so many people thought you could shovel that truth out of sight. From teenagers to politicians, too many people were eager to pretend that utopia lay just around the corner. That the world could be a place where no one ever got hurt. That was impossible, and claiming it could be done was a big, fat lie.

Still, the thing that was driving her craziest about the situation with the Voronin murals was that so many people didn't seem to see what an opportunist the head of the School Board was. Mallory had tracked down an online interview with him, and as she listened to him talk about how important it was to protect 'the precious young' from 'harm which might lead to self-harm,' she'd seen that behind all his malarkey and poppycock, his eyes were cold and hard.

Such people were very dangerous, Mallory thought. At Lyle and Cornelius's party, Matthias Mueller had said he sometimes feared he was living in an era when people would rather have enemies than friends. When people defined themselves by who they hated. Far from fighting for individual freedom, people like the head of the Bayview school board sought power over others by trying to take away the most important freedom of all – the freedom to make your own judgments and your own decisions about what to like and approve and support.

At least she and Bob would be taking the Evgeni Voronin petition to Wally and Isabella. As she turned over to go to sleep, she couldn't believe how lucky she was to have stumbled into the Jones Salvage Yard not long after she arrived in Rocky Beach – and how lucky she'd been to have been accepted the way she had been by Jupiter, Pete, and Bob.

Her only fear was that by the time next summer rolled around, they wouldn't be interested in having her hang out with them any more. She hoped she could help them solve the mystery about the falconer paintings and find a way to prove that Günther Böhm had stolen the one Per Jorgensen had given to the Center.

She and Bob had agreed to meet at the Rocky Beach Public Library and to bike together to Isabella Chang's house, and Mallory was there bright and early – though not as early as Bob. He was waiting at a table outside, and when he saw her, he jumped to his feet.

"There you are!" he said. "I called Wally and Isabella and they're expecting us. Let's go!"

It was a good ten minutes from the library to Isabella Chang's house – which lay in a part of Rocky Beach that Mallory wasn't all that familiar with. She was delighted to be with Bob and happy to finally be taking action of some sort. She hoped that doing something – even something as small as delivering these petitions – would relieve some of her pent-up anger.

She let Bob lead the way, down tree-lined streets, along the verge of a well-traveled highway, and finally to the cul-de-sac where Isabella Chang lived. Mallory was looking forward to seeing Wally Tate again. It had been a week or so now since he had moved in with Isabella, and she was eager to see how he was settling in.

As for Isabella Chang, Mallory felt as though she already knew her, although they'd never met. All three of the boys had talked about her at various times. Also, Mallory felt a personal connection to her, since it had been when The Three Investigators had been working for Isabella that Mallory, Pete, Bob, and Jupiter had met.

The street she lived on was quiet and well-shaded. Dry leaves from the magnolias rattled under their tires as Mallory and Bob came to a stop. Isabella's house looked small from the front – though Mallory thought it probably wasn't. Still, it had only one story and was sided with redwood, with a gently sloping roof and a front garden that was carefully tended. Mallory and Bob leaned their bikes against the garage and took off their helmets. Bob rang the doorbell.

It was Wally Tate who answered the door. He was humming, and he threw up his hands in mock surprise, as though they were the last people in the world he had been expecting. Mallory grinned, just seeing him. He looked very well. His blue chambray shirt had been newly ironed and his bald head glistened in the reflected light. Behind his glasses, his eyes looked warm and lively.

"I'm sorry," he said, "but I don't think we'll be needing any Girl Scout cookies this year."

Mallory laughed. "Do I look like a Girl Scout?" she asked.

Wally peered at her with interest. "Not really," he said. "And Bob certainly doesn't. Come in, come in. We've been expecting you. Isabella is sitting out back, by the koi pond."

Wally led the way. Mallory let Bob go first; after all, he'd been to the house before. She looked around her as she followed him down a hallway on which beautiful framed examples of calligraphy hung. Bob had told her about the role Isabella Chang's hobby had played in solving the case of Daniel Hernández and the forged Kit Carson letter. Hernández had been able to forge Kit Carson's signature so expertly because he also practiced calligraphy.

Wally stopped where another hallway led off to the left, and he waved airily down it. "That's my domain, down there," he said, "where I do the majority of my deep thinking. I can do my shallow thinking anywhere."

The hall opened into a sparely furnished living room, which radiated an air of serenity. A pair of lovebirds in a silver cage hung from a sturdy metal stand. Through a wall of glass, Mallory could see the back of a woman's head. She was sitting upright in a wooden outdoor chair. Her hair was silver-gray and had been gathered into a single long braid that hung down over the back of the chair.

Wally opened a sliding glass door, and the three of them entered Isabella's back yard. It was very large and very peaceful, Mallory thought. It had big borders of white calla lilies, roses, and daisies. At the back was a wooden arbor covered with yellow climbing roses, and there were big gray flagstones leading through it. The yard also had mature trees, high bushes, and a lattice fence that made it into a totally private space.

"They're here," Wally called out happily to Isabella. "And they don't seem to have changed a bit!"

Isabella laughed and turned around in her chair. Her face gave the impression of age and wisdom, but it looked to Mallory almost completely unlined, and her eyes were bright and vibrant. Bob had told Mallory that Isabella was having some trouble with her sight, but she focused immediately on Mallory's face and seemed to see her very clearly.

"Hello, dear," Isabella said. "I've been so looking forward to meeting you." She extended a warm hand. "Come right over here and take a seat. Bob, how are you?" She nodded in greeting and gave him a big smile. "Wally, would you get our guests something to eat and drink?"

"Oh no, thank you," Mallory said. "That's kind of you, but I'm sure neither of us is hungry or thirsty."

"That's right," Bob said, "Please don't go to any trouble. You'll notice that neither of us is Pete."

"All right, then," Wally said. "That's music to my ears. Most everyone I have ever known has said, 'Please go to a lot of trouble.'"

Isabella laughed again. "Since Wally moved in," she said, "I've spent half my time laughing and the other half enthralled by his wonderful stories."

Mallory was thrilled to meet Isabella, who had made her feel instantly at home without doing much at all other than holding her hand.

"So what's all this about saving Western civilization?" Wally asked.

Now Mallory laughed. Somehow, when Wally was involved, the most intense feelings were made less difficult.

"Your garden is beautiful," she said to Isabella. "A wonderful space."

Isabella nodded happily. "When I was still teaching, I had my students here for a party at the end of the school year. I understand the two of you are here because you want me and Wally to sign a petition regarding the Evgeni Voronin murals at Bayview High School!"

"Our friends Lyle Smith and Cornelius Patterson are mounting a campaign to save them," Bob said, "and one of the things they're doing is getting a lot of high school teachers to sign a petition. We wondered if either of you ever taught at Bayview."

"Not me," Wally said. "I spent my career in good old Rocky Beach."

"I never taught there," Isabella said, "but I visited it for district conferences. I've seen those murals many times. They are most impressive; you can't take your eyes off them. I'll happily sign your petition – though I'm sure everything will turn out all right even if I don't!"

Mallory could see that Isabella had the

same optimism as Jupiter, though hers seemed to flow from a generosity of spirit and a positive attitude rather than a rational approach to problems.

"I'm not at all sure everything will turn out all right," Wally said. "In my extensive experience things almost never do. But I will defer to Isabella who I'm sure knows more about these things than I."

Wally was a man after her own heart, Mallory thought.

"And from my extensive experience," Isabella said, "I'd say that the beginning of the new school year is just around the corner. Is everyone ready?"

"I hope so!" Bob said. "We've got new school clothes, and we've all chosen our sports. Mallory and I will be rock climbing, Jupiter's taking up fencing, and Pete's already a whiz at soccer. In the meantime, The Three Investigators seem to have gotten involved with one last case. Jupiter's been taking lessons in fencing at the Center for Falconry and Fencing, and the other day someone stole a painting from its lobby."

"Falconry?" Wally said. "I didn't know you could learn that in California."

"The Center is quite well known in Hollywood, I understand," Bob said, "and the Danish actor Per Jorgensen gave it a painting of a falconer to thank them for working with him."

"One doesn't often hear about falconry these days," Isabella said. "It makes me think of Yeats's poem 'The Second Coming.' Do you know it?"

When both Bob and Mallory said no, Isabella leaned back in her chair, closed her eyes, and began to recite the poem — or at least that's what Mallory thought she must be doing – from memory.

A shiver shot up Mallory's spine, right to the top of her head. "Wow!" she said. "That's really powerful."

"What's a gyre?" Bob asked.

"A spiral," Isabella replied. "The falcon has been loosed and he flies upward and away in ever widening circles, no longer in touch with the man who has trained him."

Mallory got the shivers again. She thought of what Per Jorgensen had said about falcons being afraid of nothing – but then she noticed that Wally was staring at Isabella in admiration.

"I knew there was a reason I loved you!" he exclaimed. "That's one of my favorite poems."

"Mine, too," said Isabella. "When I taught the history of the two World Wars, I always recited it to my class."

To Mallory and Bob, she explained, "W.B. Yeats wrote the poem in 1919, when the First World War had just ended and the Russian revolution had thrown that country into bloody chaos. The world seemed poised on a knife-edge. It's a visionary poem, foreseeing what would happen as the world stumbled toward World War Two."

"If I'd known you back in the day," said Wally, "I would have come and listened to your lectures!"

"You wouldn't have needed to," Isabella said, smiling. "You know as much as I do about the history of those wars – and anyway you were there for the second one."

"I remember Rafael Solares telling us that you two used to sit out on the deck of your house while you told war stories," Mallory said to Wally.

"Well," Wally said. "They weren't what I would call war stories, exactly. They were stories about things that took place during the war. I was just a kid when the war started, and everything I saw in Europe either shocked or impressed me. Now, it's easy for people to think that only the Germans were monsters, but I saw both American and French soldiers prove that war makes monsters of us all. Men in war are capable of just about anything. Women, too, I expect."

He looked at Mallory kindly, as if he didn't want to exclude her from any horrors.

"Here's a story you won't like if you happen to think that everyone on the Allied side of the Second World War was good and honorable." He paused and put his hands firmly on his knees. "One time, I was on a transport train crossing France. The train was filled with weary American soldiers and other Allied troops — French, British, Australian.

"All of a sudden there was a commotion in the front of the car, and the next thing I knew, a group of French soldiers had seized a French officer and were carrying him bodily down the aisle. He was mustachioed and wore that strange hat called a kepi that looks exactly like an oval chocolate box with a visor. He was struggling for all he was worth – kicking and flailing and yelling in French – which I don't speak. His captors were grim-faced and silent. They marched him all the way to the back of the train and then, without ceremony, they threw him off. I don't know what he did to upset them, and I don't know what happened to him."

Mallory didn't know what to say, and she could see that Bob didn't either.

Isabella, however, said, "The further we get away from that awful time, the easier it is for everything to settle into easy generalities – the Allies were all good, the Germans were all bad. But you find vicious hateful people on both sides in any war. And also people who act with honor and kindness – or who do whatever they can to thwart the hateful."

"That's very true," said Wally. "And I also have a happier story. Near the end of the war, I was sent into Czechoslovakia, and our platoon was stationed in a village where we commandeered some houses. The Germans had occupied the country since 1939, and some of the people had become Nazis out of a sense of self-protection. But others lived their lives as best they could, with a cheery sense of subversion. I got to know a bunch of musicians who were wild for American jazz – which the Germans had forbidden, of course, as degenerate. So they hid their instruments, but when they felt safe enough, out they came, and those boys could play some hot jazz.

"I knew some painters, as well, who managed to get around the German dictum against anything modern. They painted what they wanted to paint, and when they were satisfied, they simply painted over their canvases with something the Germans would approve of. After the war, they planned to remove the top painting and get back to what they had originally painted!"

"Wow!" Bob said. "That's inspiring."

"It also makes me think of the Voronin murals," Isabella said. "From what I remember, they're frescoes."

"Yes," Bob said. "That's right. Evgeni Voronin had to work very quickly, painting the murals right behind the plasterers. He had to finish the paintings before the plaster dried."

"And so they can never be painted over without losing them forever," Isabella said. "Voronin's paints actually became part of the plaster itself. If you painted over them and then tried to remove the top layer of paint, you'd take Voronin's murals with you. You said you had a petition you wanted us to sign?"

"Yes," Bob said, getting out the papers. Wally looked them over, then added a long remark to the petition page before he signed it. Isabella also added a remark, then signed the petition and handed the pages back to Bob.

While Mallory watched this happening, she found herself thinking about what Isabella had just said – and also something Wally had said earlier – with the feeling she might have missed a clue. She racked her brains to think what it might have been, but couldn't.

"Thanks so much," Bob said. "I'm so glad we came here today; spending time with the two of you is great!"

"Then you must come more often!" Isabella said. "It's always a pleasure to see you."

At that, Bob struck his forehead with his palm. "I almost forget to invite you to our birthday party! Jupiter, Pete, and I have celebrated our birthdays together ever since kindergarten, and this year, we're celebrating on Jupiter's. It's August 18th, and because we hope a lot of people will be coming, we're going to hold it at the Rocky Beach City Park."

"Well," Wally said. "Isabella and I have a very busy social schedule – "

Isabella laughed again. "We'll be there!" she said. "With pleasure!"

"I'm sorry we'll have to use a place as public as the city park, but Jupiter's house and yard just don't seem big enough right now," Bob said.

"Then why don't you have the party here?" Isabella asked. "This yard is very private. We'd love to lend it to The Three Investigators for the evening, wouldn't we, Wally?"

"I can't think of anything I'd like better," Wally said. "As long as our young friends bring the food!"

Bob looked totally surprised, but it didn't take long for him to gather his wits. "If you really mean it, that would be great," he said. "We think there might be as many as thirty people, though!"

"Twenty, thirty, or forty, they'll all be welcome!" Isabella said. "The Three Investigators have changed my life for the better, not just once but *twice* this summer" – here she looked at Wally, smiling – "and hosting a party is the least I can do for such important new friends."

"I'm sure Pete and Jupiter will be wild about the idea," Bob said, rising. Mallory rose, too.

"It was such a pleasure to meet you, Ms. Chang," Mallory said.

"The pleasure was mine," Isabella said. "And you must call me Isabella. Wally will see you out."

Which he did. "See you soon," he said,

as he closed the door.

Once it was closed, Bob glanced at his watch. "We'd better hurry. We stayed longer than I thought we would. Wasn't it great of Isabella to invite us to hold the party in her backyard?" he said as he fastened on his helmet.

"Totally great," Mallory said, fastening on hers. "And those stories Wally told about being in France and Czechoslovakia during the war were really interesting. Especially the one about Czechoslovakia."

"Yes," Bob agreed. "The story of the French officer getting thrown off the troop train by his own soldiers was more what I'd call chilling!"

It was just after noon when Mallory and Bob got to the Salvage Yard. They barely had time to get off their bikes and lean them against the office wall before Pete came running up.

"Hi, guys!" he said. "Was it great to see Wally and Isabella?"

"Yes," Bob said. "And guess what? Isabella invited us to have our birthday party in her back garden instead of the city park!"

"No way!" Pete said. "Did you say yes?"

"Of course!" said Bob. "I hope Jupiter

189

isn't mad, but I really couldn't have said no, and I didn't want to, anyway."

"It'll be great to have the party there," Pete said. "And wait 'til you hear what we found out!"

"What is it?" Bob asked.

"I better let Jupiter tell you," Pete said, "or else he *will* be mad. But we better hurry or I'll spill the beans."

Jupiter was sitting in the outdoor workshop, a pad of paper before him. He looked up at them with what seemed to Mallory a Cheshire cat smile on his face.

But before he could say anything, Pete burst out with it. "Is it O.K. with you if we have our birthday party in Isabella Chang's garden instead of at the City Park? It had better be, Jupe, because when Isabella asked if we wanted to do it, Bob said yes!"

For a moment, the Cheshire cat smile dimmed, as Jupiter pushed aside whatever he had been about to say in order to think about this news, but once he had, he said, "That was very generous of Isabella, and I'm glad that Bob accepted. Still, today our focus is on the Matthias Mueller list."

"So you had good luck with it?" Bob asked.

"Yes," Jupiter said. "We discovered two relevant facts. The first is that six of the people who bought Aksel Olsen paintings from Mr. Mueller were recently approached by an anonymous buyer who offered to pay them much more than they had originally paid for the paintings."

"Just like with Per Jorgensen!" Bob said.

"Yes," Jupiter said. "And all six of them sold the paintings, at quite a handsome profit."

"But there's more!" Pete said.

"Go ahead," Jupiter said to him. "You tell them."

"At least one other person on the list Mr. Mueller gave us was contacted about selling his painting. But he said no. And then, guess what?"

"What?" Bob asked.

"His painting was stolen!" Pete said jubilantly. "Just like the painting at the Center! Isn't that amazing?"

Wow, Mallory thought. That *was* amazing. There was no other word for it. Someone was determined to get his hands on the paintings of falconers that Aksel Olsen had done in the early 1940s, and by this time it was pretty clear who that someone was!

10

Bob Sees What Lies Beneath

Five minutes later, Bob and the others were sitting in Headquarters. The last time Bob had been in here, he, Pete and Jupiter had been planning their birthday party. This summer, they'd found themselves using the place less often than they had in the past. In fact, Bob thought, they'd almost been avoiding it since it had been broken into in the course of their case involving animal smuggling. Before that, it had always been very private, comfortable, and reassuring, but after the break-in, it had seemed less so.

Still, right now it was a better place to discuss the current case, and Bob had suggested they move in here before they talked any more. He'd been waiting all day to tell Jupiter, Pete, and Mallory what he'd discovered.

That morning, Bob and his father had been talking over breakfast about Per Jorgensen and the theft of the falconer painting from the Center, and when Bob mentioned that Günther Böhm had tried to buy a similar painting from Matthias Mueller, his father had

192

drawn Bob's attention to an article in the Arts section of the Los Angeles *Sun* – where Bob's father worked.

To increase circulation, some of the feature articles were available only in print editions, so Bob had read it in print. After Günther Böhm had crashed the fund-raising party at Matthias Mueller's house, Jupiter had told Bob and the others about some art opening Böhm had mentioned, but he hadn't been very specific and Bob was pleased to find that the article was about an art opening that very afternoon at a place called The New Resistance Co-Op, and that it contained a long interview with Günther Böhm.

Now Bob was trying to explain, from memory, what had been in the article. He wished he'd taken notes, but all he'd done was write down the name and address of the New Resistance Co-op, and he was trying to explain why it had decided on that name.

"It's off Mulberry Street," Bob said, "down an alley, and it's open to anyone who calls themselves an artist and who signs on to their basic philosophy – which, as far as I can tell, means that they have to consider most of humankind their enemies."

That made Pete laugh, but Mallory

asked, "What do you mean, exactly?"

"I mean the artists seem to think that art should be a way of protesting the oppression of one group of people by another one. I think they call themselves the New Resistance because they're trying to compare themselves to the Resistance fighters of the Second World War."

"I can't believe they'd have the audacity to do that," Jupiter said. "As we know from what happened to Aksel Olsen, the Resistance fighters of World War Two often lost their lives in service to their cause – and their cause was immediate and urgent."

"Yes," Mallory said. "To compare yourself to the Resistance fighters of World War Two takes a lot of gall."

Although Bob agreed with Mallory about this, he was eager to tell his friends the thing he'd discovered.

"Anyway," Bob went on, "Günther Böhm is one of six people whose work will be exhibited. And he's either the most famous of the bunch, or thinks he is, so the reporter focused on him."

"We should go!" Pete said. "I can't wait to see this guy!"

"I agree," Jupiter said. "This is quite serendipitous. But how will we get there?"

"Connor O'Malley's free this afternoon," Pete said. "Why don't I call him? I bet he'd be interested in going to an art opening."

"He might, at that," Jupiter said.

Bob gave Pete his cellphone and Pete called Connor. It turned out that Connor wasn't far away and could be there shortly.

"It's all set!" Pete said cheerfully, handing Bob his phone back.

"Now, back to business," Jupiter said. "What did Böhm say in the article?"

"He went on and on about how he saw life for what it really was. A terrible business, from start to finish, apparently," said Bob. "He talked about being adopted, and how that made him feel like 'a visionary internationalist,' whatever that is. He claimed to be one of only a few artists who knew how to demonstrate 'creative destruction' with his work."

"Good grief," Mallory said. "What a jackass! He must be as big a phony as the head of the Bayview High School Board."

"But what I've been dying to tell you guys all morning," Bob said, "is that he told the reporter that he'd inherited a bunch of what he called 'pretty paintings' from his father – and that he'd put a bunch of them up for auction a year and a half ago. At the firm of Hartung & Hartung in Berlin. Where Mr. Mueller bought the ten paintings of the falconers!"

Since Bob had been sitting on this information for over four hours, he was gratified to see electrified expressions sweep across the faces of his friends. Pete, of course, looked electrified quite often, but to see both Jupiter and Mallory so thrilled told Bob he hadn't been wrong about how vital this information might be.

"Did he say what the paintings he'd sold looked like, or who painted them?" Jupiter asked.

"No," Bob said. "But I bet we'll discover that the paintings Günther Böhm sold and the ones Mr. Mueller bought are the same paintings. What I can't figure out is why Böhm would be trying so hard to get back paintings he sold to begin with!"

Jupiter pinched his lower lip. "Let's not get ahead of ourselves," he said. "It's tempting to jump to the conclusion we've all jumped to. But until we know for certain who the seller of the falcon paintings actually was, we really shouldn't assume it was Günther Böhm."

"I *want* to assume it!" Pete said heatedly.

"Günther Böhm never imagined how bad his luck was running the day he ran into you! Did he strike you as dangerous when you met him?"

"No one with purple shoelaces can be dangerous," Jupiter said mildly.

Bob laughed. It was one of Jupiter's rare jokes.

"I wouldn't be too sure," said Mallory. "Sometimes the ones who seem most harmless are the least predictable when they're caught or cornered."

"A good thing to remember," Jupiter said. He paused and thought for a moment. "Although we can't yet be absolutely certain that it was Böhm who sold the ten falconer paintings through Hartung & Hartung, I wouldn't bet it wasn't. After all, it also seems significant that the Center's falconer painting was stolen soon after Böhm insisted on a tour of the place. Especially since both events occurred after Böhm was unsuccessful in his attempt to buy a falconer painting from Matthias Mueller."

"It really does seem likely that he hired the lawyer who contacted Per Jorgensen, and that he's the person who bought six of the paintings," Mallory said.

"And stole a seventh one!" Pete added.

"Or had it stolen," Jupiter said. "I'm sure it's also occurred to you that Böhm may have hired Dika Horváth. After all, Werner told us that Böhm saw her mini-trampoline the day he came into Matthias Mueller's shop, and we all agreed that the marks in the ground next to the courtyard wall at the Center were made by one."

"I *had* thought of that," Bob said. "It just makes sense."

"But to get back to your question," Jupiter said. "It really does seem puzzling that Böhm would first sell the paintings, then decide he wants them back."

"Puzzling things are what we're good at!" Pete exclaimed. "And if we're right, then Günther Böhm has now reclaimed eight of the ten that were bought by Mueller. Though he says he hates them. He went out of his way to tell you that, and Mr. Mueller confirmed it."

"Do you think he might be saying he hates them as a way to throw people off his track?" Bob asked.

"No," Jupiter said. "Günther Böhm may be cunning, but he doesn't strike me as smart. Perhaps we can find a way to discover more about his motives at this gallery opening. He certainly seems to like to talk about himself."

"Maybe I could pretend to be a journalist," Mallory said, "the way I pretended to be an aspiring history major with Daniel Hernández. He's already met you, Jupiter, but you were smart enough to keep the three of us hidden when you saw him the second time. Of course, there might be people at the opening who know about Bob and Pete and The Three Investigators. But if I stay away from you while we're there – and maybe flash a press badge or something – I might be able to get him talking. Especially if he thinks that what he says will end up in print."

"An excellent idea," Jupiter said, reaching into a drawer of the desk and pulling out a plastic card on a neck cord.

The card read *Rocky Beach High School,* and Bob remembered that he and Jupiter and Pete had all gotten one when they had visited the school the year before. It wasn't a press badge, exactly, but if Mallory pretended she worked for the Rocky Beach High School paper, it would probably do the trick.

Jupiter handed the card to Mallory, and she slipped the cord over her head.

Just then, the intercom in Headquarters squawked. "Jupiter, are you in there?" Aunt

Mathilda's voice was as loud and startling as always. "Connor O'Malley is here." Without another word the four of them scrambled out of Headquarters and into the Salvage Yard – where they all fit themselves into Connor's car once again.

The New Resistance Co-Op was a depressing place, Bob thought, when they finally got there. It had taken some work to find it. Down an alley, off a side street in an obscure corner of L.A., the place had once been a stockroom or warehouse of sorts. It was big enough for twenty artists, but the six who were using the space at the moment were clustered near the front, leaving a vast empty shadowed area at the rear.

As agreed, Mallory and Connor hung back, while Bob, Pete, and Jupiter walked in. As he looked around him, Bob saw that each so-called "artist" had between five and ten works on exhibit.

There were grainy black and white photographs of spools of thread, several ceramic pieces that looked like they had started life as vases and had collapsed, and a bunch of old treadless tires hanging from chains. The most interesting work was a series of painted portraits of women whose faces were masks of grief and sorrow, behind whom were shadowy figures wearing hooded robes.

Günther Böhm had, not surprisingly, commandeered a position near the front and in the center, where some white gypsum board partitions on rollers had been formed into a semicircle. Böhm's work, which was hanging from the partitions, looked to Bob as nonsensical as it had when he'd found pictures of it online — it was all "found" art or "arranged" art or whatever Böhm was calling it.

Scraps of paper, twigs and leaves, and, most alarmingly, strips of what looked like other peoples' paintings that had been put through a shredder had been attached to irregularly shaped canvases. They had no order, no sense of composition, and certainly no apparent purpose – except to serve as the backdrop for the written explanations which had been attached to the sides of the canvases. Bob stared at the man who was now holding forth to a small group of spectators who looked like they had come for the free drinks and food; Pete himself was eying the food table hungrily.

Böhm looked delighted, Bob thought – which was perhaps his normal state when he was the center of attention.

"My friends," he was intoning, "as a

man adopted by a family of Nazis, I can tell you from personal experience just how hard and ugly the world can be – ” when Mallory and Connor appeared on the other side of the small group of people. Bob could see Connor recoil from the art on display; he was clearly offended and dismayed.

Mallory was waving her hand, which made her fake press pass sway on her chest.

“Excuse me, Mr. Böhm,” she said. “I’m from the Rocky Beach High School paper, and I’d like to ask you some questions.”

Böhm paused mid-sentence and gazed at Mallory. He seemed to be asking himself if she were really a reporter and decided to err on the side of caution. He also seemed, surprisingly, to know what a Scottish accent sounded like.

“Ah, young lady, young dasher-about-town, did you come all the way from Scotland to interview me?”

“Actually, no,” Mallory said. “I just came down from Rocky Beach.”

“And where is that delightfully-named hamlet?”

“It’s up the coast,” Mallory said. “I read your interview in the Los Angeles *Sun*, and I thought an article about you aimed at younger people would be great for the first edition of the new school year."

"Ah," Böhm said. "Reaching the young. What a fine idea. Ask away! I have nothing to hide!" He laughed merrily, as if the people surrounding him might think he actually *did* have something to hide. Which he did, Bob thought. Or at least he hoped he did.

"You said to the reporter at the *Sun* that you didn't like pretty pictures," Mallory continued. "Is that true?"

"Of course I don't like pretty pictures," Günther Böhm said. "This is an ugly world, alas."

"And the pictures you talked about in the paper?" Mallory asked. "The ones you sold at the auction house in Berlin? What were they like?"

"Oh, those," Günther Böhm said dismissively. "I inherited them from my adoptive father, who in turn inherited them from *his* father – the Nazi officer I mentioned. I myself would have sold them immediately, of course, but when they made their way back to Germany in 1945, I was just a gleam in the eye of the universe, and my grandmother kept them. She thought there must be an interesting story behind them."

To Bob, watching and listening closely,

there seemed a change in tone when Böhm arrived at the sentence about the interesting story. This made sense, he thought, if Böhm had just recently realized that his grandmother had been right.

"If I could ask about your work," Mallory said. "Why do you include bits and pieces of other people's art in yours?"

"You should look more carefully, my dear young lady," Günther Böhm said. "I do not include bits and pieces. The entire work is bits and pieces. Nothing from me but the brilliance of the arrangement! But to answer your question directly, my work reveals that nothing can ever last. In such a world, destruction is better than creation!"

Bob watched as a half-frown crossed Günther Böhm's face. "I don't know whether or not I mentioned to the reporter that my grandfather owned a painting by the Norwegian Edvard Munch – a painting stolen during the Second War. He reported the theft to the authorities at the time, and if the work is ever recovered, it will come to me. Now *there* will be a painting worth destroying!"

He chuckled happily.

"Which reminds me of my next venture," he added. "You may have heard of the current brouhaha surrounding the murals by that socialist realist Voronin. I have contacted the president of the school board which plans to destroy the murals, and I am hoping he will permit me to pick up the pieces of plaster and carry them away after the others have wielded sledgehammers and pick axes!"

Bob looked at Mallory, afraid that this latest outrage would prove too much for her, but somehow she was managing to maintain her self-control and the persona of a journalist.

Not so Connor O'Malley, who was now growling in rage. Bob was afraid he was about to physically attack Böhm.

"That's very interesting," Mallory said. "But you still haven't answered my earlier question. You haven't told me what the paintings you auctioned off were actually like."

"What they were like?" Böhm said. "They were boring and predictable and ordinary. They were paintings by some unknown and now forgotten minor talent. Nothing I would care to destroy."

Bob could see that Böhm was so impressed by the sound of his own voice that he could have gone on spewing words for hours, but Mallory wouldn't let him simply keep talking.

"Excuse me," she said, "but perhaps my question was badly phrased. Could you describe the paintings you put up for auction?"

Böhm looked around him in exasperation, raking the faces of his small audience as if looking for support. It seemed to Bob that his gaze stopped for a minute when he came to Jupiter, as though he were trying to remember if he had ever seen that face before. Bob suspected that, like most criminals of the blustery sort, Böhm talked too much and listened too little and didn't look closely enough at other people.

Nevertheless, Bob saw a look cross his face that he hadn't seen before – an uncertain, cautious look, as if he had suddenly remembered that he did, indeed, have something to hide. He stared above the heads of the people he'd been talking to, up into the cavernous reaches of that old warehouse.

"Describe them?" Böhm repeated. "Why, each of them alone would have been bad enough, but the endless repetition – They were, um, they were paintings of — how can I describe them?"

He paused again before continuing with a sly smile.

"They were paintings of a lovely medieval lady in a long flowing gown. And she was carrying a bird cage made of, made of willow twigs, and in some of the paintings the cage was empty, and in some there was a pert little songbird in the cage. Does that satisfy your curiosity, my dear young lady?" he asked Mallory pointedly.

"Yes, thank you very much," she said. "Just one more question."

She raised her finger as if about to draw the question on the air when the door of the New Resistance Co-op flew open behind her, and five black-clad figures rushed in. Their faces were obscured by black bandanas they had fastened over their noses and mouths so that only their eyes were visible, and they each carried a paper cup.

They ignored Günther Böhm, who looked up expectantly – sure they had come to see him – and rushed up the side of the warehouse toward the exhibit of the paintings of grieving women that Bob had admired earlier.

"End the oppression of women!" one of them screamed. "No more tears! We want rage!"

Without pausing, they flung the contents of their cups at the crying women on the wall, and Bob was shocked to see that they had con-

207

tained paint — black and red — that now dripped down the women's faces. Someone hit a fire alarm and the place was inundated with clanging and ringing. The noise was so extreme that Bob put his hands to his ears. As soon as the alarm sounded, the black-clad figures disappeared as quickly as they had arrived, leaving behind trails of paint.

What in the world was this about? Bob wondered. Who were these masked people? Then he heard two of the other spectators talking. From what Bob gathered, the black-clad group had splintered off from the Resistance because it wasn't sufficiently violent and radical. They were resisting the Resistance. They had turned their former friends into enemies. And more art had been destroyed.

The woman whose paintings had been attacked was crying, and as someone managed to shut the alarm off, the noise of her crying echoed through the building. The other artists whose work was being shown all rushed to comfort her – all except Günther Böhm who turned to the people he'd been speaking to and said, "Well, where were we?"

At another time, Bob might have been shocked by the callousness and insensitivity of the man, but at the moment, he was still thinking of how amazingly effective Mallory had been in getting Böhm to reveal that the paintings he had sold had, indeed, been the paintings of the falconers.

But as he looked back at the red and black paint dripping down the shadowed canvases in the corner, and saw the crying woman trying to blot the paint off other paint, he stopped dead in his tracks.

Of course! he thought. Ever since Wally had told him and Mallory the story about the artists he'd met in Czechoslovakia who had painted over their own art, a thought had been trying to make its way to the surface of his consciousness, and as it finally did, Bob felt as though he'd been punched in the chest.

In fact, the revelation of why Günther Böhm was almost certainly trying to get the falconer paintings back hit him like a thunderbolt.

Bob had just turned to Pete and Jupiter to tell them what he'd finally deduced when he felt someone touch his arm, and he turned to see Mallory.

"You were great!" Pete told her. "You could be a real reporter if you wanted!"

Mallory shook her head, smiling. "I have to hand it to Günther Böhm. I didn't think he was smart enough to transform ten medieval falconers into ten medieval ladies with songbirds!" she said.

"He managed to see his own danger in time," said Jupiter, "but even so, there's no longer any real doubt that Böhm was the anonymous seller at the Hartung & Hartung sale. Well, we've gotten what we came for, and I think we can get out of here before the police come."

As they all turned to leave The New Resistance Co-Op, Bob took one last look at the defaced canvases and their distraught creator. Although he had to wait to get into Connor's car to share the revelation with his friends, as soon as they were settled – and before Connor turned the engine on – Bob spoke.

"Don't drive away just yet!" he said, his voice tense with excitement. "I just figured out what's been going on! The big question has been if Böhm sold those ten Aksel Olsen paintings, why would he want them back badly enough to steal two of them and pay thousands of dollars for the rest? Because there must be other paintings beneath Aksel Olsen's! Probably paintings the Nazis would have confiscated and destroyed if they hadn't been covered with portraits of Bjørn Kalberg! Paintings Böhm didn't know about when he sold them, but that he somehow figured out about later."

Before Bob had even finished talking, both Mallory and Jupiter were loudly exclaiming.

"Of course!" Mallory said. "I knew that Wally and Isabella had given us a clue. I just couldn't think what it was!"

As for Jupiter, he looked embarrassed. "I'm an idiot! I should have known the moment Werner mentioned Huganay! But what's this about Wally and Isabella?"

"This morning Wally told us a story about some artists he met in Europe," Mallory said, "who had painted what the Nazis would have considered "degenerate art," then covered it over with more conventional paintings. At the end of the war they planned to strip the top painting off! You can do that if paintings are on canvas, though not if they're on plaster."

"Huganay! Of course!" said Pete. "And really, we *all* were idiots!" When Mallory looked a little baffled, he said to her, "In our second case ever, we found a painting that had had another one painted over it!"

Connor O'Malley had been sitting with his hands on the wheel of his car, just listening hard. But now he said, "I'd like to wring that

Günther Böhm jerk's neck for his plans to use the pieces of the Voronin murals and the Munch painting in his wretched junk. In fact, if I'd stayed in that so-called 'New Resistance Co-Op' a moment longer, I would have turned the Böhm jerk himself into junk! I hope you four can figure out how to stop him from destroying other people's work. And what paintings *are* under the Aksel Olsens?"

"We can't know for certain yet," Jupiter said, "but I've been thinking about those letters on the gauntlets of the falconers, and with the help of Bob's brilliant deduction, I would hypothesize that they may be the initials of a group of early twentieth century artists – the ones whose work has been painted over."

"You mean the initials stand for their names?" Pete said in high excitement. "I bet you're right!"

Bob, as always, was impressed with the quality of Jupiter's thinking. Wally's story and a crying artist dabbing paint from the surface of her canvas had let Bob crack the secret of why Böhm wanted the Aksel Olsen paintings, but he hadn't leapt ahead to this other insight.

Now, as he thought about the pictures he and Mallory and Jupiter had found online, he said in a hushed voice, "Wasn't one of those sets of initials EM?"

"It certainly was," said Mallory. "Edvard Munch! You said that madman would never get his hands on that painting, Jupiter."

"I did," Jupiter said. "And now it is up to us to make sure that he doesn't. We can only assume that a man as indiscreet and bombastic as Günther Böhm wouldn't have been able to keep it a secret if he'd already found it. And I think it's time to pay a visit to the Haldorssons – to ask Freya to translate the letters between her grandfather and Bjørn Kalberg!"

A Family Tale Explained

The next morning, Pete was up, showered, and dressed by eight o'clock. A year or two ago he wouldn't have thought he could get all that interested in a case that mainly involved art, but he was eager to get to the Haldorssons, to see the eleventh painting, and to hear what Freya might reveal to them about the letters between her grandfather and Bjørn Kalberg.

The night before, after they'd gotten back to the Salvage Yard, Bob had called Freya on the speakerphone in Headquarters to tell her what they'd discovered. When he'd asked if they could come over the next day so she could translate the letters, she'd been delighted. Even though it was the weekend, her brothers needed to work. Which was good, she said. If they were hanging around while she translated, she was sure they'd quibble with her translation.

After calling Freya, Bob had also called Worthington to see if he could take The Three Investigators and Mallory to Palisade Point.

Now, the five of them were on their way, and after Jupiter had filled Worthington in on the details of their current investigation, Worthington told them proudly that his new business – as a chauffeur-for-hire at a moment's notice – was picking up nicely.

"Gee, Worthington," Pete said. "That's great news!"

"Yes, indeed, Pete," Worthington said. "When were you planning to schedule your last fencing lesson, Jupiter? I want to be sure I reserve the time."

"I've penciled it in for the morning of our birthday party," Jupiter said. "I hope that by then we'll have found the Munch and snared Günther Böhm."

"Very good, Master Jones," said Worthington, smiling.

"And then school starts!" Pete said. "But even though we're not planning to solve cases during our freshman year, we want to stay in touch with you, Worthington."

"Never fear, Pete," Worthington said. "Never fear."

Worthington had no trouble finding the Haldorssons' house. Even to Pete, who knew next to nothing about architecture, the house looked Scandinavian. It had a steeply pitched

roof and a small balcony on the second floor
from which long trails of vines with yellow flowers hung. It was painted grayish-green and
brown – two colors Pete wasn't used to seeing
in California, but which went really well together, he thought.

As they got out of the Flex, Pete saw
Freya waving gaily from a stone terrace to the
side of the house. He thought she looked quite
dressed up for a Saturday. Worthington elected
to stay with the Flex, so Pete and the others
made their way over to Freya.

"I'm so glad you could come," she said,
and though she was saying it to all of them, she
was looking intently at Bob. "I want to show
you where I planted the geraniums you gave
me," she added.

Bob glanced at the others, a slightly
worried look on his face, but he let himself be
ushered to a small patch of plants in a sunny
corner of the backyard.

"I think somebody likes somebody," Pete
said, smiling.

Inside, they found that both of Freya's
parents were home. Mrs. Haldorsson was red-
cheeked like her daughter, but Pete was most
fascinated by the way her hair had been
braided and then coiled on top of her head.

Mr. Haldorsson was an orthopedic surgeon, Pete learned, and though he was on-call that weekend, he seemed relaxed and happy to meet them all. He looked remarkably like his sons — handsome and blond and wiry. He had a reddish beard.

"I think first," Freya said, "we should take a look at the painting of Bjørn Kalberg," and she led the way to the dining room, a long room with windows on one side. The other side featured a number of works of art – among which was the Aksel Olsen.

This was the first time that Pete had seen one of his paintings in person — he'd seen the photograph that Mr. Hutchinson had given them, and the thumbnails online, but none of them had prepared him for the effect of the real thing.

The falconer and the falcon seemed so life-like that Pete wouldn't have been surprised if the falcon had suddenly cried in alarm or if Kalberg stepped out of the painting and introduced himself.

"Yes," Mr. Haldorsson said. "That is my father's friend. I met him when he was quite a bit older, years after the war. They had been friends since childhood."

"Like us!" Pete said. "We met in kindergarten.”

“Old friends are the best friends,” Mr. Haldorsson said.

“But sometimes new friends can be just as good,” Bob said. Although Pete was pretty certain Bob was referring to Mallory, he could see that Freya thought the reference was to her, and he wished Bob would be a little more careful.

“Look,” Jupiter said, pointing to the falconer’s gauntlet. “No letters. No initials. That clearly suggests this is simply a portrait of Kalberg and not a painting hiding another painting beneath it.”

“I wonder why Olsen would have painted another portrait of his friend,” Bob said. “You’d think he‘d have tired of the subject by then.”

“Maybe there’ll be information in the letters,” Freya said hopefully.

“Freya has told us what you’ve discovered,” Mr. Haldorsson said, “and it is fascinating. As for your question of why Olsen painted yet one more portrait of Kalberg, perhaps he did it as thanks for sitting for the other portraits, and also for his help in keeping the original paintings out of the hands of the Nazis. Then he gave it to him as a keepsake. A memento.”

Wow! Pete thought. Another memento. It seemed he wasn’t the only one who liked mementos!

“We’ll leave you young people to yourselves,” Mrs. Haldorsson said. “We need more coffee! Freya, let us know when you all go up to the attic.”

“Yes, mama,” Freya said, and Mr. and Mrs. Haldorsson retreated to the kitchen as Freya took Pete and the others into the living room.

“Here is the hand loom my brothers made,” Freya said.

“Awesome!” Pete said. “That’s really great!” The loom was made of four highly polished lengths of wood, joined at the corners so they made a rectangle a little over two feet high and about a foot-and-a-half wide. The background of the piece Freya was weaving was blue and green, and just beginning to take shape.

At the bottom were two claws grasping a branch.

“It’s going to be a falcon,” Freya said proudly. “Or at least I hope so! Do you want to look at my grandfather’s letters now?”

“Very much,” Jupiter said.

"I'll just tell my mother," Freya said, and she called to the kitchen that they were off to the attic.

The wooden staircase from the second floor up to the attic was narrow and the handrails were splintery. There was a trapdoor of sorts that Freya threw back and then all of them were standing on a wood floor to which nothing had been done in some time. It was a bit dim, as the only light came from the windows in the gable ends, but it smelled wonderfully of heated wood and dry air.

A big worktable had been set up at one of the gable ends to take advantage of the light, and Freya gathered them round as she took the top off a large wooden box. She removed the first thing on top – a binder with plasticine sleeves.

"These are the pressed flowers my grandfather made. I told you he was a gardener! I don't have any idea how old the flowers are, but they were all grown in Norway." She looked at Bob, who was busy taking out his notebook and pen in order to record all important information.

"Maybe we can look at them later," Jupiter said. "Right now, we should get to the correspondence."

"Of course," Freya said. She started pulling piles of letters from the box and putting them on the table.

"Gosh!" Mallory said. "There are a lot of them. Maybe we should organize them by author and date, then interweave them so we can get some sense of a dialogue between your grandfather and Kalberg."

"An excellent idea," Jupiter said approvingly.

"And we should make sure that we keep the envelopes together with the letters they contained," Bob added – at which Freya hurried downstairs to her bedroom and came back with a plastic container filled with colored paper clips.

They all pitched in, taking the letters from their envelopes and paper-clipping them together, then scrutinizing them for their dates and signatures. Soon they were building four piles — letters from Håkon Haldorsson written before the war; letters he wrote after the war was over; and two corresponding piles for Bjørn Kalberg.

Pete had a little trouble figuring out the dates, since, he discovered, Europeans put the day of the month before the name of the month, and when they just used numbers for the month, everything could easily get backwards.

But soon they were putting the letters in each pile in chronological order, and then going back and forth between Haldorsson and Kalberg, interweaving the letters to make a correspondence. As it turned out, though the two friends had written a few letters during the war, the vast majority had been sent in the three years that followed it.

"What do they say?" Pete asked excitedly.

"Well," Freya said. "This will take a little time." She picked one up at random. "God dag, min gode venn," she read. "Good day, my good friend."

Pete groaned.

"I'm afraid most of what they wrote won't be of much help to you," Freya said. "I should have read them all earlier so I could have pulled out the ones with information."

"Well, there's no time like the present," Jupiter said.

And so Freya began skimming her grandfather's letters and the letters of his friend.

"That one is about someone getting married," she told them, putting it firmly at the end of the table. When she found a letter that seemed relevant, she translated it carefully, and if she ran into a Norwegian word she didn't know, she looked it up in her Norwegian-English dictionary.

Pete appreciated how conscientiously she was doing this, but he had to admit the speed at which the investigation was proceeding was driving him a bit crazy. He was starting to think there must be nothing relevant in the letters when Freya suddenly said, "Here's something about the paintings!"

Everyone settled down and listened carefully.

"Aksel har gjort en veldig god jobb," Freya began. "I'm sorry — Kalberg is writing that Aksel Olsen has done a very good job with the paintings. He goes on to say that he has never seen something so, so genuine that is actually –." She paused. "Forfalsket. There's a word I don't know in English."

She picked up her dictionary and started thumbing through it. "Here it is," she said. "Forfalsket. Factitious."

"Fac- what?" Pete asked.

"Factitious," Freya repeated.

"That's great," Bob said. "You look up a word in the dictionary, and it gives you a definition you have to look up, too. Does anyone know what 'factitious' means?" He looked to Jupiter and Mallory but neither one of them could help. "O.K.," he said. "Time to get serious." As Pete watched, Bob took his laptop out of his bag, booted it up, and typed 'factitious' into the search bar.

"Here we go," Bob said. "'Factitious' means 'falsified; artificially created or developed; bogus; fake; counterfeit.'"

"That certainly makes sense in the context," Mallory said. "Kalberg wrote that Olsen had made a painting that looked real but was really bogus — because of what it was hiding."

"The entry goes on to say that the word 'factitious' is sometimes used with more abstract ideas – like identity," Bob said. "So it's actually a pretty good word in this context, because that's what all three of them were doing. I mean, you could say that Freya's grandfather, Kalberg, and Olsen had all created factitious identities when they concealed from the Nazis that they were actually members of the Norwegian Resistance."

"Yes," Mallory agreed, "and as we found out, maintaining that factitious identity was a matter of life or death."

"And here's an interesting sidelight!" Bob went on. "In Danish, as a verb, *at forfalske* means to forge a document or a painting!"

While the other four had been talking about the word "factitious" in many variations and several languages, Freya had just kept looking for more letters which might be relevant to the investigation, and now she said, "Oh my gosh. Here's a letter from Kalberg to Grandfather about the German officer he taught falconry to."

"The German officer he was also spying on," Jupiter said.

"Yes," Freya said. "But this confirms they also became friends." She read for a while in silence.

"His first name was Klaus," she told them, "and he was an *Oberstrichter*, Kalberg writes. A lawyer, I guess, but what my brothers told you was right. He had a special role as something called 'a cultural liaison officer.' Kalberg says that he'd been encouraged to bring his own paintings and books and records with him to Oslo. He says that the Nazis inventoried everything, so the Third Reich knew exactly what he had brought with him from Germany."

"The Nazis were great record-keepers,"

Bob said. "Fanatical to the point of insanity. Order, order order; lists, lists; lists."

"It's hard to piece all this together," Freya said, looking from letter to letter, "but I'll try my best."

Half an hour later, what had emerged, to Pete's astonishment, was what Mallory called a tale of high intrigue and subterfuge. The letters confirmed that because falconry was now a sport of the elite, the German officer had decided to learn it to better ingratiate himself with the Norwegian upper class. This was how he'd met Bjørn Kalberg, and although he had no way of knowing that Kalberg worked with the Resistance, it didn't really matter, as the two of them had become friends.

The new and exciting information was that the German officer had eventually confided in Kalberg that he was becoming more and more nervous about ten of the paintings he had brought with him from Germany − because he knew the Nazis considered them "degenerate art." Other Nazis were in and out of his house all the time, and he was afraid that the paintings would be seized and destroyed one day.

So together with Bjørn Kalberg and his artist friend Aksel Olsen, the German devised a plan. One night when no one was watching, he and Bjørn Kalberg had carried the ten paintings out of his house and into the back of a box truck, and they had driven the truck to Aksel Olsen's studio. There, they had hidden the paintings, and in the days that followed, Bjørn Kalberg had dressed up like a medieval falconer and posed for the painting which was now in Freya's parents' living room.

Aksel Olsen had used the first painting as the model for all the other paintings he had painted – although, of course, in the case of the others, he was painting over the paintings removed from the German officer's house. To keep track of which painting was which, Aksel Olsen had painted the initials of the artist whose work lay under his own on the falconer's gauntlet – and because the Nazis knew he had previously owned them, the German officer had reported that the ten "degenerate" paintings had been stolen.

However, as soon as a bit of time had passed, the counterfeit paintings had been returned to the German officer so that he could take them back with him to Germany and have them stripped, once the war was over. The "stolen" paintings would be safe!

"What an amazing story!" Pete said.

"Too bad the story itself got lost somewhere along the way!"

"Does the German officer's name appear anywhere in the letters?" Jupiter asked Freya. "It would be very helpful if it did, because although all of us are probably thinking the same thing, we really have no proof yet that the officer was Günther Böhm's grandfather. Or, rather, as Günther Böhm himself would put it, the father of the man who adopted him!"

"Bjørn Kalberg just referred to him by his first name – Klaus – I guess because he and Klaus were really friends," Freya said. "When you're talking to friends about friends, you don't usually mention their last names."

"Did you find anything else, Freya?" Mallory asked.

"Just this letter from the end of their correspondence," Freya said. "It's very sad and mournful, about how much Kalberg misses Aksel Olsen. It's several years after Olsen's execution, but Kalberg still feels it keenly. He says he's very glad to have a painting of himself done by his friend. He says that, if he dies first, he will leave it in his will to Grandfather."

When she looked up from this last letter, there were tears in her eyes, and Pete could see that Bob really wanted to comfort her. However, in the end it was Mallory who put her arm around Freya's shoulder, saying, "I know how you feel. Those men were brave. They are worth crying for. By anyone. And you can be very proud that one of them was your grandfather."

Freya looked up at Mallory gratefully, and then everyone helped her put the letters back in the envelopes they belonged in.

"I guess you'll be going now," said Freya.

"I'd actually like Bob or Mallory to do a bit of research before we leave," Jupiter said. "Even though all we have is the name Klaus, the way the Internet works, that name – linked to Böhm – might be a lot of help. Bob, since your laptop's out, could you look that name up, along with Norway and 1945?" Jupiter asked.

Pete watched as Bob typed "Klaus Böhm" into the search bar and then scanned the article he found – an article posted on the website of the Norwegian-American society.

"He *was* Günther Böhm's grandfather," Bob said excitedly. "He *had* to be. It says that a German officer named Klaus Böhm who was stationed in Oslo during the Occupation died under mysterious circumstances, right after the German troops surrendered to the Allies. There was a rumor he'd been killed by an American."

"He was murdered?" Freya asked.

"That would be true if the rumor were true," Jupiter said.

"There was no proof," Bob said. "But it seems he had made a lot of friends in Oslo who saw to it that he had a proper funeral and burial and a proper gravestone. He's buried in an Oslo cemetery. The article mentions that he had a son back in Germany, Siegfried Böhm, who later made a fortune through the mining and selling of potash."

"The German industrialist who adopted Günther!" Jupiter said. "Now all we need is to find a list of the ten supposedly 'degenerate' paintings Klaus Böhm owned, stole from himself, and had painted over in Aksel Olsen's studio!"

"When I was doing research the other day in the Salvage Yard," Mallory said, "I discovered an inventory of still-missing paintings stolen or lost during the Second World War. It's the all-Europe alert list, so that galleries and auction houses won't be selling work that actually belongs to somebody else."

With Mallory's help, Bob found the list

quickly enough; it was sorted by artist, the name of the painting, and the original owner. When Bob typed Klaus Böhm into the database, he came up with a list of ten paintings and thumbnails of those for which photographs had been found. As Pete peered over his shoulder, he saw that the very first painting on the list was "The Village" by Edvard Munch.

Pete whooped at the top of his lungs, and even Bob and Mallory and Freya made pretty loud noises. But while the noises were partly noises of pride and satisfaction, they were also noises of worry, and when everyone had quieted down, Jupiter pinched his lower lip.

"So," Jupiter said. "We now know for certain that the ten paintings that Günther Böhm put up for auction at Hartung & Hartung had originally belonged to his grandfather, Klaus Böhm, who had been stationed in Norway and who had contrived, with two members of the Norwegian Resistance, to save ten "degenerate" paintings he was afraid might be seized and destroyed by his confederates. After Klaus Böhm died, the ten hidden paintings were returned to his widow in Germany, but without the story of what they really were."

"I remember Böhm saying at the Co-Op that his grandmother thought there must be an interesting story about them," Mallory said. "Boy, was she ever right!"

"Her grandson, who hated the paintings and wanted to get rid of them, unsuspectingly sold them, not knowing that at least one of the paintings – the Munch – was worth a small fortune," Jupiter said.

"Not that he cared about that!" Mallory said. "He just wanted the publicity he'd gain from destroying it!"

"The big question," Jupiter said, "is what to do next. The painting downstairs is safe, but Böhm is still after the last two on the Mueller list. If we can, we should track down the owner we couldn't find yesterday and warn him. And we need to see Matthias Mueller right away. He may be the person who actually owns the Munch! And he may be in danger of losing it at any moment!"

12

An Urgent Mission

It was ten minutes later, and The Three Investigators and Mallory had said goodbye and thank you to the Haldorssons and rejoined Worthington in the Flex. As they left Palisade Point, heading for Los Angeles and Matthias Mueller's store, Worthington was driving within the speed limit, as always, but today Jupiter wished that, just this once, he would throw caution to the winds and step on it. He felt an urgency he couldn't explain. It was almost as though he feared that, just at that moment, Günther Böhm was getting his hands on the Munch. Out the window, cars on the other side of the highway sped by.

Jupiter tried to calm himself with the rational thought that, even if Worthington risked a ticket by going five or even ten miles faster, they would save at most two or three minutes. But after five more minutes of driving, he asked Worthington to pull off the highway and find somewhere where Bob could make a phone call they could all hear. Worthington did as he was asked, and soon Jupiter, Pete, Bob, and Mal-

233

lory were sitting at a picnic table under the spreading shade of a California sycamore.

There, Bob set his cellphone in the middle of the table, turned the volume up to high, and dialed the number of Matthias Mueller Limited. The phone rang and rang – three times, four times. Was the gallery open today? It was a Saturday, wasn't it?

On the sixth ring, a familiar female voice said, "Matthias Mueller's. How may I help you?"

"Dika," Jupiter said. "Is that you? This is Jupiter Jones from The Three Investigators. Is Mr. Mueller there today?"

"I think he just stepped out for a sandwich," Dika said. "Oh, no, my mistake, there he is. Just a moment."

Jupiter heard the sound of the receiver being dropped, and then the ambient noise of the gallery — humming silence interrupted by faint voices he couldn't decipher. He looked above him to the leaves of the sycamore turning softly in a light breeze. His three friends were all staring at him expectantly. Bob was sitting on his hands; Mallory had clasped hers before her; and Pete was on the edge of the bench, his arms crossed on his chest. He smiled at them, but they all looked anxious.

After an interminably long time, a voice said, "Jupiter?" It was Matthias Mueller, at last.

"Mr. Mueller," Jupiter said. "I'm sorry to bother you at work, but this is very urgent. I'm afraid you have no idea what it is you really bought at auction at Hartung & Hartung a year and a half ago."

"What do you mean?" Mueller said, his voice suddenly very interested.

"Before I say anything more," Jupiter said. "Is there someplace you can go in the gallery where you won't be overheard?"

"Certainly," Mr. Mueller said. "Just let me walk to my office at the back. This sounds serious!"

"It is," Jupiter said. "We've discovered that Günther Böhm's grandfather was a Wehrmacht officer who owned ten paintings he was afraid his Nazi confederates might seize and destroy because they were considered 'degenerate art.' His name was Klaus Böhm, and he and a Norwegian friend who was teaching him falconry arranged to have the painter Aksel Olsen paint over the paintings, to protect them. So while the ten paintings you bought looked like portraits of a medieval falconer, under that top layer of paint were ten

235

works by painters Hitler hated, or disapproved of."

"I always knew there was something about those paintings! Can this be true, though?" Mueller asked. He sounded both mystified and excited.

"And there's more," Jupiter said. "Aksel Olsen wove a secret code into the paintings. He painted the initials of the original painter on the falconer's gauntlet. Do you remember what initials are on the gauntlet of the painting you refused to sell to Günther Böhm?"

"Of course," said Mueller. "The initials are EM."

A gasp went round the picnic table.

"Then I have the pleasure to inform you," Jupiter said, with suppressed excitement, "that you are actually in possession of a canvas painted by Edvard Munch in 1880, before he entered his expressionist period."

"A Munch!" Mueller exclaimed incredulously. His voice had suddenly gotten very high and it vibrated with excitement.

"Yes, indeed," Jupiter said. "It's called 'Village Scene.' We've looked it up online; it's been missing since the Second World War and it's listed both on a site devoted to Munch and on the database of paintings that were stolen or that otherwise disappeared during the war. In this case, however, the painting wasn't actually stolen."

"A Munch!" Mueller said again. "And not only that, but the very Munch Günther Böhm talked about in my shop! Why, this is astonishing news!"

From his voice and tone, Jupiter and the others could tell that the painting was, for the moment, safe, and that they could stop worrying that Böhm was about to seize it.

"Unfortunately," Jupiter said, "that is the painting that Günther Böhm is most fanatically after. He has systematically tracked down and either bought back or had stolen each of the other paintings you acquired from Hartung & Hartung, with two exceptions – your painting and one other we've been unable to find."

"And to think that if he had been less obnoxious, or if I had been in a different mood, I might have sold it to him!" Mueller said. "He might have destroyed it by now!"

"At any rate," Jupiter said. "I do not think it is safe merely hanging on the wall in your house."

"No, no," Mueller said. "I quite understand. I'll leave at once, go home, box it up, and take it to a vault I have access to where I can keep it safe until Böhm is secured and can do no further harm."

"The problem is, I'm not sure exactly how to stop him," Jupiter said. "He has mostly stayed inside the law, though in the case of two of the paintings – including the one stolen from the Center For Falconry and Fencing – he is an accessory to theft — though he did not do the actual stealing himself."

"Who did?" Mueller asked.

Jupiter looked at the others and both Bob and Mallory shook their heads in an emphatic no.

"Now is not the time to tell you that, Mr. Mueller," Jupiter said. "It would be far better if you took the steps you outlined to keep the Munch safe."

"Yes, yes, I will," Mr. Mueller said. "I'm very grateful for your help. I have to say that when Werner told me about the interview he'd read in which The Three Investigators were mentioned, I was a bit doubtful, but now I am a total believer!"

"Thank you," Jupiter said, with some satisfaction.

Jupiter was just about to bring the conversation to an end when Mr. Mueller began speaking again.

"By the way," he said. "I've just thought of something. Last spring — late May, I think — I was contacted by one of the curators for European art at Hartung & Hartung. It seems that during transport from wherever they had been stored, one of the falconer paintings had been damaged. The bottom right-hand corner was badly scratched or abraded, I don't know. On examination, they discovered some sort of unusual priming on the canvas — not the normal white of gesso you might expect."

"Yes," Jupiter said. "That would make sense. The damage uncovered part of the original painting!"

"Hartung & Hartung had an art restorer repair the canvas from photographs taken before the damage was done, and the woman told me that Hartung & Hartung had intended to inform both the seller and whoever was bidding on the paintings about the damage and restoration. But somehow this information was never conveyed. Now, over a year later, they were trying to make up for their mistake."

"That is very interesting," Jupiter said.

"At the time," Mueller said, "I made nothing of it and merely thanked the woman. It never occurred to me that there was another painting under the Olsen painting — just as it never occurred to anyone at Hartung & Hartung."

"But it occurred to Günther Böhm," Jupiter said. "And I would bet he was tempted to hit himself in the head when he deduced that the 'pretty paintings' were much more valuable than he had ever imagined – that he had sold ten paintings he now very much wanted to get back. Because he knew that his grandfather had had a Munch, and now that it was missing, logic suggested it was among the ten."

"And if Hartung & Hartung informed Böhm at the time they informed me," Mueller said, "then that explains why he suddenly appeared in Los Angeles earlier this summer, pretending he was here to exhibit his so-called art when what he really was doing was trying to reacquire the paintings!"

"Thank you very much for thinking to tell me this story," Jupiter said. "It explains something that's been bothering me – how and why Böhm came to understand the mistake he had made in auctioning off the paintings to begin with!"

"Well, I had better be going," Mueller said. "I have a Munch to protect. Thank you once again, Jupiter. I am forever in your firm's debt."

"Goodbye, Mr. Mueller," Jupiter said. "We'll be in touch again when there is any news."

He watched Bob end the call and return the phone to his pocket. The constricted feeling in Jupiter's chest that had begun in the Haldorssons' attic was now subsiding. He was surprised at how personally he was taking the case. If someone two weeks ago had asked him a theoretical question about how he would feel about works of art being preserved, he wouldn't have known how to react; he hadn't really thought about it. Now he knew how important it was. He felt personally responsible for the Munch.

"Well, that's that," he said. "Now all we have to do is figure out how to prove what Günther Böhm has been up to, and get him to stop it. Let's go back to the Salvage Yard and come up with a plan."

They all piled back into the car, and on the way to the Salvage Yard, they talked. Before they'd left the Haldorssons, Jupiter had had time for just a quick look at pictures of the ten paintings Klaus Böhm had saved from possible destruction. The painting stolen from the Center had covered a painting by someone named Heinrich Tellerman. Hidden underneath Aksel Olsen's portrait of Bjørn Kalberg was a painting of very dubious value – at least in Jupiter's opinion – and now he asked the others what they had thought of it.

"Was that the one with black lines running back and forth, making a series of boxes, some painted in and some empty?" Bob asked. "I thought it was pretty bad."

"It looked like an imitation," Mallory said. "I don't know the name of the painter whose work that guy was copying, but the imitation was terrible."

"I agree," Jupiter said. "The painting that Aksel Olsen put on top of it is of far more interest and beauty."

"Now that Günther Böhm has his hands on it, I sure hope he hasn't stripped off the Olsen painting yet," Bob said.

"Yikes!" Pete said. "I hadn't thought of that. We promised Per Jorgensen we'd get the Center's painting back!"

"There's no use getting worried when we don't know what's happened yet," Bob said. "Maybe Böhm has been so intent on getting all the paintings that he hasn't had time to see what's underneath. Besides, as we all know, the painting he's really after is the Munch."

"Yes," said Jupiter. "But if Böhm had

figured out the code in the gauntlets, why would he have purchased and stolen so many paintings just to secure a single one of them?"

"Oh, no, you're right!" said Pete.

"It's very lucky that Mr. and Mrs. Haldorsson have the original Aksel Olsen portrait of Bjørn Kalberg," Jupiter said. "It would be a shame if all of that work was erased from the world forever."

For the rest of the ride back to the Salvage Yard, there was silence as they all contemplated this final comment, and when they arrived, everyone jumped out as if their clothes were on fire. They called a hello out to Aunt Mathilda, then hurried to the outdoor workshop. Bob took out his computer and continued his exploration of the site with the list of stolen paintings, but Mallory simply sat and thought.

Though she didn't pinch her lower lip the way he did, Jupiter had come to notice the signs – a somewhat blank expression, eyes that seemed to be focused on something not immediately apparent. Meanwhile, Pete was practically bouncing in his chair.

Jupiter said, "I think the key to the situation may be Dika Horváth. She was the one who actually stole the painting from the Center, and probably from the private home as well. But she didn't strike me as incapable of reason. Perhaps if we confront her with what we know, and assure her we'll do everything we can to keep her out of jail, she'll do what she can to help us get Böhm."

"Great idea!" Pete said. "And there's no time to waste! Even though the Munch is safe, I really want to try to get the Center's painting back before Böhm has a chance to strip it."

"I agree with you that someone should talk to Dika," Mallory said. "But even if she's older than we are, the four of us together will seem pretty intimidating. Maybe I should approach her by myself. She's certainly not dangerous."

"No," Jupiter said, nodding, "I would agree with that."

"But how can she help us?" Bob asked.

"I don't know," Mallory said. "I'm just working this out as I go. What we really want to do is to catch Böhm breaking the law. So how could we get Dika to help us do that? Maybe − ." She paused and collected her thoughts, then picked up a green wooden box she had found in a shed somewhere and held it on her lap. As she peered into it, she started talking.

"I think I've got it," she said. "If I can

get Dika to confess, maybe I can also get her to help set up a sort of sting. As of now, there's a falconer painting out there somewhere whose owner you couldn't track down, and if you couldn't find it, there's every reason to believe that Böhm couldn't find it either. So he'd be ripe for false information about where that last painting is.

"Maybe I could get Dika to inform him that the buyer died soon after buying the painting from Mr. Mueller, and that the painting now belongs to someone else — through an estate sale or something – . I don't know."

Jupiter found himself more and more impressed with Mallory. She sounded surprisingly like him when he talked aloud – to himself or to one of his friends – trying to work things out.

"O.K., O.K.," Mallory said. Jupiter could see her mind whirring, and it was a bit disconcerting. Was this what he looked like, some of the time?

"So," Mallory went on, "Böhm knows there are two paintings he hasn't gotten his hands on, and though he probably suspects that the painting Mueller wouldn't sell to him is now at Mueller's house, he doesn't know if that painting is 'Village Scene' or a painting he has no real interest in. If Dika told him that the missing painting had the initials **EM** on the falconer's gauntlet, that she had tracked it down, and that it now belonged to a specific person from whom he could steal it, he'd be thrilled."

Mallory stopped and looked straight at Jupiter.

"And that person could be Per Jorgensen," she added.

A jolt of something like electricity ran through Jupiter. He felt fully, totally focused.

"Yes," Mallory said, as if to herself. "This is good. If she agrees, we could have Dika tell Günther Böhm that Per Jorgensen was so upset by the theft of the painting he'd given to the Center that he'd asked an assistant to see if he could find one of the other falconer paintings to replace it. His assistant managed to discover that one of them was being offered at an estate sale, and Per Jorgensen bought it. The sting would involve Dika convincing Böhm to steal it from Per Jorgensen's house."

Mallory's face shone with excitement and pleasure as she came to the end of her thought. Jupiter could see how much she wanted to make a major contribution to the case, and she just had! Her plan could really work. Though she'd helped a great deal in unmasking the forger and charlatan Daniel

Hernández in their second case that summer, he knew how badly she'd felt when her mother had forbidden her from being in on the trap that led to his arrest. She'd missed their third case entirely, and although she'd been crucial in their fourth one, in the last case – up in Isla Vista – she somehow felt she hadn't done enough. This time around she wanted to help out in a big way.

"I have to tell you, Mallory," Jupiter said. "I'm impressed with your plan and I truly believe it will work. The first thing we need to do is to call Per Jorgensen and ask for his help, and the second is for you to convince Dika to work with us to sell the lie to Günther Böhm."

"You're right, Jupe," Bob said. "We need to catch Böhm in the act. He may be devious and obnoxious, but he got the majority of the paintings fair and square by paying for them."

"But couldn't Dika just tell the police what he got her to do?" Pete asked.

"She could," Mallory said. "But remember it was Dika who did the stealing. Anyway, the Munch will be too important to him. He'll want to be there."

"I can't wait to expose him," Bob said.

"Me, either," said Mallory.

Jupiter suggested, and everyone agreed, that when Pete got home later he should call Per Jorgensen and see if he'd agree to help trap Günther Böhm.

"I'm sure he will!" Pete said. "He said he'd help us in any way he could. And this way, he'll really be involved in getting back the painting he bought for the Center." He closed his eyes and crossed his fingers. "Hoping, hoping, hoping it's still all right," he said.

"Here," Bob said. He took from his wallet the card that Per Jorgensen had given the boys at the conclusion of their visit.

"Thanks!" Pete said. He put it safely in the pocket of his shirt.

"So let us know as soon as you talk to him," Jupiter said. "If he agrees, then Mallory can go to Mr. Mueller's gallery on Monday morning and talk to Dika. In the meantime, why don't we see if we can get Werner to find out anything from Dika that might be helpful or useful to Mallory? They've worked together for most of the summer, and surely she won't get suspicious if Werner asks her a few questions. Bob, would you call him?"

"Sure," Bob said. "I'd be happy to. And I'll also suggest the sorts of things he might want to ask and the things he might avoid, so as not to raise her suspicions."

"All right, then," Jupiter said. "I think the four of us have had quite an eventful day. All the pieces of the puzzle are in place, at last. We finally understand everyone's motives and their actions – and not just in the present, but also during the war some seventy-five years ago. The courage Böhm's grandfather, Kalberg, and Aksel Olsen showed should be an inspiration to us. They were falconers – or maybe falcons – all of them. So, I'll see you guys soon! Why don't we lay low tomorrow and get some rest. This case has been exhausting; we've been all over the map!"

Mallory, Bob, and Pete had ridden over to the Salvage Yard on their bikes that morning, and Jupiter waved as they each mounted and took off for home. As the last one rounded the corner and disappeared, he turned and walked across the Salvage Yard toward his house.

Up in his bedroom, he was about to lie down for a short rest when a glint of glittery purple caught his eye. There, on the windowsill, where he'd placed it days before, was the matchbook that Günther Böhm had unceremoniously dropped outside the Center for Falconry and Fencing the day that Jupiter had met him. He couldn't believe he'd completely forgotten about it, and now he picked it up and opened it.

Why had he never even tried to dial the telephone number Böhm had written inside?

Well, he thought, he could still do it.

The house was empty. Aunt Mathilda was in the Salvage Yard's office, and who knew where Uncle Titus was? In the kitchen, Jupiter picked up the phone and dialed the number. He knew from the +49 that the number was international – Germany, he supposed – and he listened to it ring, three short bursts followed by silence followed by three more short bursts, disconcertingly unlike the ringing of an American telephone number.

As Jupiter listened to the ringing, he suddenly remembered that it was late in the evening in Germany, and that whoever he was calling might be awakened by his call. He was about to hang up when an answering machine picked up and Jupiter heard a melodious female voice saying, "Hartung & Hartung, Kunst und Auktionen" followed by some words in German he didn't understand, but that he assumed meant he should leave a message.

He hung up, sat down at his desk, and stared at the matchbook, twirling it in his fingers. Böhm had written down the number of Hartung & Hartung. But when? Before the auction of the ten paintings he'd given them? After they'd contacted him about the unusual priming they'd found?

Jupiter was a methodical and logical thinker; he examined the clues as they came to him and put them in their proper place. He stared, aghast, at the matchbook, hardly believing he had overlooked it, hadn't followed up on it. He had been careless. This was a clue he should have pursued long before.

Jupiter thought he would find a place to put the matchbook so that he saw it often, so that it would serve as a reminder to him that he could not get lackadaisical or lazy. The case would have proceeded much more quickly – or at least he might have gotten to the heart of the matter earlier – if he had known that Günther Böhm had written the number of an auction house in Germany in the matchbook!

13

A Plea To Dika Horváth

Late Monday morning, Mallory sat alone in the living room of her apartment in the Wessex House, a big Victorian that had been divided into apartments some years before. When they had first arrived in Rocky Beach, Mallory hadn't thought she would like living in such close proximity to other people, but the apartment was not only bright and airy, with high ceilings and great bay windows, but also quiet and private.

She particularly loved her bedroom. There, under the window, she had put the immigrant's trunk with her name painted on it that The Three Investigators had given her as a present after her help with their first case of the summer. Every time she looked at it, she felt happy.

Worthington was coming to drive her to Matthias Mueller's gallery any minute. She was quite excited, because her plan of Saturday was beginning to take shape. Pete had called to tell her that Per Jorgensen had agreed to help, and Bob had called to say that Werner

Mueller had managed to get Dika to admit that she had "done some work" for Böhm. That was the wedge that Mallory would use to get her to admit more about what she'd been up to.

Mallory smiled when she remembered Pete's call. According to him, not only was Per Jorgensen eager to help; he would be very much like the character he'd played in *The Seventh Messenger* – strong, courageous, ruthless. Mallory could almost hear the swoosh of his double-bladed sword!

With Per Jorgensen on board and with Werner's help, Mallory was feeling optimistic. She was thrilled at the thought of catching Günther Böhm red-handed and exposing him for the charlatan and fraud he was. It would be almost as satisfying – though Mallory had to admit, not quite – as exposing the head of the school board, with his plan to destroy the Voronin murals.

She glanced at her watch. Worthington wouldn't get there for a few more minutes. Thinking about *The Seventh Messenger* had brought the image of a falcon into her mind, so she opened her laptop, typed "falconry" into her search bar, and began to read about its long and complex history. She was interested to discover the ways in which the sport had had an impact on the English language.

For example, "hoodwink" – to fool or deceive – seemed to have come from the practice of calming a falcon by putting a hood over its head, so it couldn't see what was around it. "Fed up" had derived from the fact that falcons wouldn't want to hunt because they'd already eaten – and that hunger was what generally drove them. And "under one's thumb" was thought to refer to the jesses or leather straps attached to the falcon's legs being held tight in the falconer's hand.

As she thought about these phrases, Mallory was startled by a knock on the apartment's door. She quickly closed her laptop. Worthington! She rushed to the door and opened it to see the tall, handsome man she had come to feel so fond of. He had been extremely kind all summer – referring to them as fellow expatriates from Great Britain. He had brought her and her immigrant's trunk back to the apartment the day The Three Investigators had presented it to her, and he had even shooed off her dreadful cousin Skinny Norris.

She was happy to see him, and he seemed truly happy to see her as well. This ride would be special, because usually when she saw

Worthington it was as part of a group. Before she left the apartment, she grabbed the Voronin petitions that Wally and Isabella had signed; this would be a good chance to deliver them to Mr. Mueller.

The ride to Mueller's gallery took longer than she had expected, somehow, but as they drove, Mallory and Worthington talked about the summer now almost over, and all the many changes it had brought. It had begun with Mallory's arrival in Rocky Beach. Not long afterwards, Worthington had quit his job at the Rent-'n'-Ride Agency, where he'd driven the Rolls-Royce that had first introduced him to The Three Investigators, and had begun his own business. Then the boys had bought the Flex with the reward money from Isabella Chang. He and Mallory could hardly keep up with all the driving Worthington had done for them, and all the adventures he'd been part of.

As they got nearer to Los Angeles, Worthington asked her about the unfolding plan to catch Günther Böhm, and she explained it — though she found it a little difficult to explain Günther Böhm himself.

"I know that The Three Investigators have run into a number of pretty bad people in their cases, but although this guy doesn't *seem* as bad as some of them, to me, he actually is. For one thing, he's done nothing with his life – absolutely *nothing* but criticize other people and the world he lives in."

"The lure of doing nothing is that you can do it perfectly," said Worthington. "If you actually *do* something, you are bound to be imperfect – to make mistakes you can't explain away."

Mallory was struck by the wisdom of this remark. "That's really true," she said. "And the other thing that gets me about him is that he seems to feel he's actually better than everyone else."

"The two things go together," said Worthington. "If you contribute nothing to society except a constant stream of criticism, it's easy to feel morally and intellectually superior."

"Morally superior!" said Mallory, snorting. "He has the gall to think of himself as an artist when he's really a thief and a liar and a talentless bombastic boor!"

Worthington laughed, and said, "Well, I'm sure you and the boys will find a way to knock him off his self-constructed pedestal!"

"I hope so," Mallory said. "But if we do, Dika Horváth is going to have to help us."

With that, the two of them fell silent. It

was another bright California morning, though Mallory could judge the subtle changes in the angle of the sun as the season edged toward fall. Its rays glanced off the storefronts less urgently, she thought.

Worthington pulled up in front of Matthias Mueller Limited, and Mallory got out. "Thanks so much, Worthington," Mallory said.

"Not at all," Worthington said. "I'll be parked very close. Come looking for me when you're finished."

Mallory opened the tall gilt-lettered door and entered the cavernous space of Mr. Mueller's gallery, with its high tin ceiling and its polished wood floors and its wall of paintings, lithographs, drawings, and etchings. It took a moment for her eyes to adjust to the interior light, and she stood uncertainly by the door. But Bob had told Werner that Mallory would be coming, and Werner had told his uncle, so Matthias Mueller was looking out for her arrival.

"Mallory," he said, walking up to her and shaking her hand warmly. "It's good to see you again." Together, they walked toward his office.

"You, too, Mr. Mueller," Mallory said.

He was looking dapper today, she thought, in a gray lightweight herringbone suit. His shoes had been polished until they shone. "Before I forget, here are those petitions you gave us, signed by two wonderful retired teachers."

Mueller took the petitions and set them on a pile on his desk.

"Did you secure the painting?" she asked.

"Yes," Mueller said in a lowered voice, looking around to see where in the gallery Dika Horváth was. "I've gotten it locked away in an art vault. No one is going near it until I go to get it!"

"I've seen photos of it online," Mallory said, "but I'm sure they will be nothing compared to the original. How will you go about revealing it?"

"I've taken some photographs of the Aksel Olsen painting already, but before I have it stripped, I plan to have high-quality professional photographs taken, so that I can contribute the images to digital databases that track these things. I wouldn't want Aksel Olsen's work to be completely lost – even though that was clearly what he intended to happen.

"Then, luckily, we happen to know the

very best art restorer in all of Southern California – maybe in all of California! Cornelius Patterson will know exactly how to remove Olsen's paint from the canvas while leaving the Munch intact. It will be a long and laborious process, but he will do an excellent job. I can't wait to watch him work, and to see the Munch gradually appear."

"I know what you mean," Mallory said. "Do you think that Jupiter, Pete, Bob, and I could watch at least at little of the process, too?"

"Of course!" Mr. Mueller said. "But first we need to catch Günther Böhm – and I take it you've had some good ideas about how to do that."

"I hope so," Mallory said. "Jupiter didn't tell you on the phone who we suspect helped Böhm steal the paintings, but by now Werner has surely told you. Dika raised Jupiter's suspicions right from the start. It seemed odd that Werner was sure she'd met Günther Böhm, but she tried to pretend she hadn't. Now that she's admitted that she's done what she called "a little work" for him, I'm hoping to get her to admit what that work was, and how deeply she's involved."

"I've discovered something that may

help you do that," Mr. Mueller said. "I've been looking into Dika's status in the United States, and it appears that her work permit expired last June. I don't want to blackmail Dika with this information, but although I was very disappointed in her, when Werner told me what was suspected, I now think that perhaps the reason she did what she did was that Günther Böhm had somehow stumbled on the same information."

"That makes total sense," Mallory said. "In fact, it explains everything." As she said this, it occurred to her that three might be better than one in the coming conversation. "Would you and Werner be willing to help me get Dika to confess, and then to persuade her to help us catch Günther Böhm in the act?"

"I would," Mr. Mueller said, "and I'm sure Werner would! Let me make sure we are not interrupted."

He had no customers at the moment, so he strode briskly to the front of the gallery and flipped the sign on the door from OPEN to CLOSED. While he was doing so, Werner appeared from wherever he had been, and when he saw her, he waved merrily.

"Hallo, hallo!" he called as he walked over to her, nodding.

"Thank you for talking to Dika," Mallory said. "Your uncle and you and I are all going to see what else she has to tell us."

"Excellent!" Werner said. "We will investigate!"

Mallory followed Mr. Mueller and Werner toward the back of the gallery where Dika sat at a long table going over some forms. She looked up with a pleasant expression. With her cropped hair, her black leggings, and her coiled energy, she seemed very much like a gymnast, Mallory thought.

"Could we speak with you for a moment, Dika?" Mr. Mueller asked.

An expression crossed Dika's face that was hard to interpret, Mallory thought. But it seemed clear that she knew something was up.

They all repaired to Matthias Mueller's office space, a large ornate old oak desk at the very back of the shop. Because one of the gallery's walls was on an alley, there were windows and natural light, and the place seemed to Mallory quite open and non-threatening. Out the nearest window she could see people walking by, intent on conversation.

"Won't you sit down?" Mueller said to Dika as he settled himself on the edge of his desk and gestured toward one of the folding chairs in front of him. Werner and Mallory took chairs to either side of Dika. She seemed a little tense, but under the circumstances, Mallory thought, remarkably cool and calm.

Mr. Mueller cleared his throat and looked at Dika kindly. "I'm sure you remember Mallory MacLeod," he said. "She has some questions to ask you today."

Mallory gathered her thoughts before speaking. "The second time we met, you pretended you didn't remember who the German artist Günther Böhm was, but I understand from Werner that you've actually done a little work for him. Is that true?" she asked.

"Yes," Dika said grudgingly. "A little."

"What sort of work?" Mallory asked.

Dika looked startled. Finally she said, "A bit of gymnastic work."

"Can you be more specific?" Mr. Mueller asked. "We really want to help you, but I've been looking into your status here in the United States, and it seems to me – please correct me if I'm wrong – that your work permit expired last June."

Dika looked panicked, and then she nodded, once, and got very still.

"Are you going to turn me in?" she asked. "I like it here. I have been trying to fit in. I haven't been making any trouble."

"That's not strictly true, though, is it?" Mallory said.

"I thought you might be more understanding, since you were not born in this country, Mr. Mueller," Dika said. "And neither were you, I think," she added, turning to Mallory.

"Actually, I was," Mallory said, "though I grew up in Scotland. Still, I know what you mean, and we don't want to turn you in. But if you mean by "gymnastic work" that you've been helping Günther Böhm steal falconer paintings in order to stay in this country, maybe you'd like to help *us* now – this time by getting him to steal one too many!"

"One too many?" Dika asked, looking confused.

"We'd like you to help us set a trap for him – a trap in which he tries to steal another painting and is caught."

At this, Dika looked interested. "But how would I do that, exactly? And would you pay me, as Günther Böhm has?"

"Günther Böhm paid you to steal the paintings?" Mallory asked. Up until now, she'd been feeling very sympathetic to Dika, but when Dika mentioned being paid by that ghastly phony artist, Mallory no longer felt any sympathy at all.

"Well, he hasn't paid me yet, of course," Dika said. "He said he would only give me the money when all ten paintings were in his hands."

"And do you think that money justifies outright theft?" Mr. Mueller asked sternly.

Dika looked at him as though that was a very strange question.

"Maybe not," Dika said. "But money is very important. It does not make you happy or well if you are sick, but I have found that there is a great difference between having money and not having any."

All three of them looked at her in silence. "You have to understand that Günther Böhm bought six of the paintings, and as far as I could see, the few people who would not sell to him were just being stubborn, because he offered them money, too – much more than they paid to you, Mr. Mueller," she said.

When no one responded to this comment, either, Dika went on, very earnestly, "But he was not just going to steal the paintings from them. He promised me that afterwards he would be sure they got the money they would have gotten if he had bought them.

So they were not so bad off and I did not think it was particularly bad to help him in this way."

This made Mallory more than a little skeptical. "You believed him? That after he stole their painting he would send them money? Why would he do that?"

"He said he would," Dika insisted, "though you do make it sound silly. Anyway, I certainly never liked him, and I will help you in any way I can. You do not need to pay me; it will be payment enough to get out from under Günther Böhm's thumb − though afterwards, I will need to return to Romania, I suppose − which will be a very big shame. What do you want me to do, then?"

"Before I get into that, could you tell us what you've done so far?" Mallory asked.

"The first thing that happened was that he wanted a list of the people who had bought the paintings from Mr. Mueller's shop, so I went into the computer and printed it off. Werner taught me how."

Both Mallory and Mr. Mueller turned to Werner. He looked surprised.

"What?" Werner said. "I did not."

"No, early in the summer, remember? When we were looking for the customer who bought the lithograph by Escher because we had gotten another one? I watched you as you found the name."

"And you remembered how I did it," Werner said.

"Yes," Dika said. "I'm a — how do you say it? — quick study. But so is Böhm. He saw my mini-trampoline the day he came to the gallery, sized me up, and said I looked like a gymnast. Later he said he could use someone with my skills to help him get the paintings from the people who would not sell them. By that time, he had told me that the paintings he really wanted were underneath the paintings you could see. He said that the paintings were lost masterpieces he was going to restore to the world."

As Dika talked, she seemed to warm to her task, and Mallory thought that her eyes took on a particular shine.

"And stealing the paintings, it was very exciting," she said. "More exciting than working in a gallery and selling paintings to women who want to match their sofas. Although I've always loved paintings, many of the customers who come to this store are not exactly looking for a painting by Nicolae Grigorescu."

Mr. Mueller harrumphed.

"It is true!" Dika said. "I got to use my

gymnastic skills, vaulting up onto the wall of the courtyard of that strange Center place. Climbing up the drainpipe of that man's house. I was not doing any damage, really. I was not throwing things around or breaking things or leaving a mess. I was just going in quickly to find the painting and then to bring it back out. No damage done. Well, I did have to break that one pane of glass in the man's house to open the window, but that was all."

Mallory imagined Dika vaulting from the mini-trampoline up to the wall of the Center's courtyard; she imagined her doing a series of backflips and leaping twists, balancing on a balance beam, swinging on the uneven bars.

"You sound almost proud of what you did," Werner said.

"And why shouldn't I be?" Dika said defiantly. "I am a very good gymnast, and it was good to see I still had all my skills. And no one saw me, or caught me."

Mallory hardly knew what to say to this – particularly because just a few weeks before, she and Jupiter had *also* been proud when they had climbed into the window of a warehouse in Isla Vista, scouted it out, and escaped back through the window without being caught or seen. Her sympathy for Dika had returned, and now, when Dika said, "So what is it that you want me to do?", she was happy to take her time explaining the plan she had come up with on Saturday.

"We want you to tell Böhm that the painting he hasn't been able to track down has been bought by the man who gave the painting to the Center For Falconry and Fencing. His name is Per Jorgensen, and you should tell Böhm that Jorgensen plans to give the Center this second painting as a replacement for the first one."

"So that he will want to steal the painting from the man," Dika said.

"Exactly," said Mallory. "Per Jorgensen is quite a well-known Danish actor who is making a name for himself in American movies. You can tell Böhm that Mr. Jorgensen is away from home at the moment, shooting a new movie, and that the house will be empty."

"That is good," Dika said. "That will make things easier. Is he really away?"

"No," Mallory said, grinning. "He will be waiting for Günther Böhm, along with me and The Three Investigators."

"Ha ha!" Dika said. "Very funny. You must give me his address, and also your phone number, and I will give you mine. Then, as soon as I know what night we will try to steal the painting, I will call and tell you."

"There's one other thing," Mallory said. "Not all of the paintings under the falconer paintings would really qualify as lost master-pieces, but one of them certainly would. It's a painting by the Norwegian artist Edvard Munch, and it's the painting he really wants to get his hands on — and *not* to restore it to the world, but to destroy it."

"Destroy it?" Dika said, aghast.

"Yes," said Mallory. "And as it turns out, there was a code painted in the falconer paintings — a code in which the initials of the original artist were displayed on the gauntlet of the falconer."

"Yes," said Dika. "He found that out very late."

"If you tell Böhm that the initials on the painting in Per Jorgensen's house are EM — for Edvard Munch — he will want to get to the house — and the painting — as quickly as hu-manly possible!"

"Very good," said Dika nodding.

Dika and Mallory exchanged phone numbers, and Mallory took a hard look in Dika's eyes. Was she trustworthy? She had worked for Mr. Mueller and yet had helped a

man she knew her employer distrusted and disliked. Yes, the man had threatened to report
her to Immigration. But she had also confessed
to liking part of what she did for him.

Mallory thought it was possible that she
would go and tell Böhm the truth, that The
Three Investigators were on to him, and that
would allow him to elude them. So it all came
down to Dika doing what she had said she
would do. Mallory would not know for sure until she got the phone call from Dika, telling her
that the sting was on.

Still, everything Dika had said and done
during their meeting had convinced Mallory
that although they came from very different
backgrounds, she and Dika weren't really as
different as all that — and the way she had
looked when Mallory told her that Böhm
planned to destroy the lost Munch if he could
get his hands on it had been highly reassuring.

"So!" Mr. Mueller said. "That is good!
Now it is past time that I re-open the shop.
Everyone to work!"

Mallory shook everyone's hand and
thanked Mr. Mueller and Werner for all their
help.

"Call us with news!" Werner said, and
Mallory promised him she would.

Worthington had found a parking space not too far from Mueller's gallery, and Mallory had no trouble finding him, though once again it was disconcerting to move from the quiet, dim interior of the gallery to the noise and smells and harsh sunlight of Los Angeles. She slid into the Flex next to Worthington. He had been reading a newspaper, which he folded carefully before turning to her.

"How did it go?" he asked.

"Really well, I think," Mallory told him. "Dika has agreed to help us − or at least I think she's agreed."

"If you trust her," Worthington said, "then I'm sure it will all work out."

"I *think* I trust her," Mallory said, as Worthington began the drive back to Rocky Beach. The two of them fell silent, and as she watched the world rushing toward her through the windshield, she remembered Dika saying that she would love to get out from under Günther Böhm's thumb. That reminded Mallory of what she'd read that morning about falconry and the English language. Now she thought it might be fun to use what she'd learned in a sentence.

She thought this sentence out, then decided it would run as follows: "Although Mallory and her friends were totally fed up with Günther Böhm and all other charlatans and phonies and inauthentic people, Böhm would soon be hoodwinked by Dika's story and soon after that – with any luck – he'd be under The Three Investigators' thumb."

If it really happened like that, Mallory could feel that she'd made up for her somewhat underwhelming contribution to their previous investigation!

14

A Real-Life Photo Shoot

The next two days were very busy, but late in the day on Wednesday – two days after Mallory had managed to persuade Dika Horváth to help The Three Investigators capture Günther Böhm – Bob sat in the middle of the back seat of the Flex between Jupiter and Pete. They were on their way to Per Jorgensen's, and out the window to the west, Bob could see the molten orange ball of sun as it sank slowly toward the Pacific Ocean – though it was a little awkward for him to see it clearly.

Why did he always get the middle? Mallory was in the front, next to Leif, who was driving. When Leif had heard about the plan, he'd offered to drive them again. Not only did he want to be part of the action, but he wanted to see Per Jorgensen again!

As for Mallory, she'd been in a state of some uncertainty since she'd talked with Dika at Matthias Mueller's gallery, so she'd been happy when Dika had called her that morning to say that she and Günther Böhm would be going to Per Jorgensen's house that evening, after dark.

Luckily, when he'd heard about the plan, Per Jorgensen had really gotten into the idea of catching Günther Böhm in the act. In fact, he'd immediately thought that there ought to be something hanging on the wall for Böhm to properly "steal." Since Matthias Mueller had told Mallory that he'd taken a photograph of Aksel Olsen's painting before putting it in the vault, she'd called the dealer and asked him to enlarge the photograph to the dimensions of the original, and then to frame it.

Per Jorgensen had gone to pick it up.

Since Pete has been the person talking about all this to Per Jorgensen, he knew what had happened next, and was happily reporting the details to his friends and Leif.

"So the photograph is hanging on his wall right now," Pete said, "where anybody who breaks in will see it right away. And he's set up cameras to catch Böhm in the act!"

"How will it work?" Bob asked Pete, but it was Jupiter who answered him.

"As I understand it," Jupiter said, "the set up is quite sophisticated. Mr. Jorgensen got in touch with one of his contacts in the photography department of the studio that shot *The Seventh Messenger*. He came by the house to coordinate everything. There's now a hidden video camera focused on the imitation painting, and it will be running when Böhm enters the house. That will give us a record of everything Böhm does and says inside."

"But the best part is the other camera!" Pete said.

Jupiter smiled. "Yes, indeed," he said. "There's another camera – a big box camera – on a tripod, also focused on the painting, as if Jorgensen was about to photograph it and then got interrupted. It will be quite obvious, but also as Böhm sees it, quite harmless."

"But it's not harmless at all!" Pete said.

"That's right," Jupiter said. "It's attached to a motion sensor, and as soon as that sensor is tripped, the camera will take a flash photo every two seconds for a solid minute. We should get thirty still photos of Böhm and Dika caught in the act."

In the front seat Mallory chuckled grimly. "Let's see Böhm try to get out of that!"

"The one thing we still don't know," Jupiter said, "is how Böhm will react to being apprehended. He's unpredictable. He could fight like a cornered animal, or he could turn tail and try to run."

"I vote he's a spineless, lily-livered

coward," Pete said.

"We won't know until it happens," Jupiter said, "so no one should get overconfident."

"Ho!" Leif said. "I would not worry too much. There will be six of us, and only one of him."

That was true, Bob thought, but even so, you could never really know how these things would turn out. He remembered the look of shock on Daniel Hernández's face when he, Pete, Jupiter, and Pete's father had materialized out of the darkness of Phillipa Paxton's house in their second case of the summer – and how glad he'd been that Mr. Crenshaw had been there to overpower Hernández. Still, he reflected, with two grown men and the four of them, Böhm wasn't going anywhere – just as Leif had said.

Bob had come up with a plan of his own that he wanted to bring up and talk through with everyone as soon as they'd gotten to Jorgensen's house. For the time being, it could wait.

As they came around a bend in the highway, the rays of the setting sun caught the raven atop Per Jorgensen's totem pole, making it look as though it were about to take flight.

"There it is!" Pete said, just as he had

the last time.

Leif managed to slow down safely and turn onto the rutted dirt driveway to Per Jorgensen's cabin. When they arrived, Per Jorgensen was out in the driveway, holding Brigitte on a leash. He was dressed in dark colors — black jeans and a navy blue tee shirt — and when darkness fell, he would be barely visible, Bob thought.

When Leif came to a stop, Per Jorgensen went over to the driver's side window and spoke to him.

"There's room for the car in the garage," he said. "Let everyone out and then park next to the Jeep."

Ahead, at the end of the drive, Bob could see a concrete pad with a small weathered garage made of the same gray wood as the house. He and the other three got out, and Leif glided into the garage next to Per Jorgensen's Jeep. He came out, and Per Jorgensen lowered the garage door.

"There!" he said. "No cars! No one home! Now come with me. I want to show you where we all will be hiding."

Nestled between the house and the garage was a small wooden structure, plain and gray. Bob could see it was a woodshed, stacked with what looked to be cedar and pine, cut neatly into lengths to fit Per Jorgensen's fireplace.

As Jorgensen brought them over, he said, "Welcome to my Günther Böhm blind."

"Your what?" Pete asked.

"You've heard of a deer blind or a duck blind?" Jorgensen asked. "A place where hunters can hide so that the animal they're hunting cannot see them and will come closer? So! My Günther Böhm blind!"

"That's great!" Pete said. "He certainly will be blind to what's about to happen!"

Bob could see that the shed was ideal for the purpose. It faced the driveway, so that they would be able to see anything that came down it, but it also had an ample view of the house. And because it was only half-full of wood, there was plenty of space for all six of them. And Brigitte!

"Will Brigitte bark?" Pete asked. "Maybe she'll give us all away."

"Do not worry about Brigitte," Per Jorgensen said. "If I tell her to be quiet, she will be quiet. She is very well-trained. Now come into the house so I can show what I've got set up."

The view out of the wall of windows facing the ocean was breathtaking and stopped

Bob in his tracks for a moment.

Jorgensen then showed them the photographic reproduction of the falconer painting hanging on the wall, not far from the front door. It looked almost real, Bob, thought − especially in the dimming light. Facing it, about ten feet away, but with its lens focused on the "painting," was a large box camera on a tripod. It looked exactly as though the photographer had just finished preparations for a photo shoot and had stepped out for a minute.

"And over here," Jorgensen said, "is the video." His friend had positioned the camera so that it would catch anyone coming through the door and approaching the Olsen "painting." It was cleverly hidden among books in a stand-alone bookcase that had been moved to function as a sort of room partition. Bob was very impressed.

"We still have a little time before darkness falls," Jorgensen said. "Why don't we go down to the sand to watch the sunset?"

He let Brigitte off-leash, and she dashed out the open sliding glass door, onto the deck, down the steps, and then sat waiting at the top of the path leading to the beach. Jorgensen strolled after her, as did Bob and the others, and soon they were down on the beach.

Bob could never watch the sun sink into the ocean without a sense of wonder. Although it looked as though its fire were being extinguished, it was actually ninety-three million miles away from any water. As it began to slip under the rim of the world, its roundness seemed to flatten, becoming oblong, and streaks of molten red-orange spread across the horizon. The colors were reflected in the ocean and seemed to be streaming toward them on waves of ripples.

"Crikey!" Mallory said. "What a view you have!"

"Yes. I'm lucky," Per Jorgensen said. They settled themselves on the sand, arms around their knees. Though the beach still held the heat from the day's sun, it cooled rapidly, and Bob could feel the chilliness seep into him. The sun had now just disappeared, and the sky was suffused with bands of cantaloupe and pink. Higher up, in the dome of the sky, darker bands of blue were gathering.

Bob looked over at Mallory who was staring out at the slowly darkening ocean with a look of deep contentment. He was truly happy for her – happy that this had all worked out so well. He knew that she liked him and

Pete and Jupiter and was happy to have them as her friends. But he also understood that it wasn't enough for her simply to hang out with the Three Investigators. She had to earn her keep, as it were – to be truly useful to their investigations. And this trap for Günther Böhm had been her idea, from start to finish.

Nevertheless, it was one thing to set a trap and quite another to catch the prey. They did not have Günther Böhm quite yet. And besides that, Bob had been worried about how they'd both nab Böhm and keep Dika out of trouble.

Now he spoke up. "I had an idea earlier today," he said earnestly. He cleared his throat and began again. "I'm sure we'd all agree that what's most important is stopping Günther Böhm from doing what he's doing — spreading nonsense, shredding or destroying other peoples' art, and then calling it his own. I think that's more important than sending him to jail. If that's what happens, he'll just think of himself as a hero or a martyr and he'll try to manipulate the situation to make himself even more notorious – the artist as outlaw or something. He'd probably only serve a small jail sentence, and when he came out he'd be worse than he was before!"

"You're right," Mallory said. "In fact, going to jail would fit right into the story he's telling about himself. Though he certainly wouldn't like it much."

"The police haven't really gotten involved so far," Bob went on, "except for that cursory investigation they did at the Center. So maybe we could give Böhm a choice – either he changes his ways, or he goes to jail. After all, unlike Böhm, The Three Investigators know the difference between an enemy and an adversary!"

Jupiter smiled at Bob remembering what he had said at Lyle and Cornelius's party.

"How would we know he'd changed his ways, though?" Pete asked.

Bob opened his backpack and removed a sheaf of papers from it.

"I wrote up a simple confession for him to sign. It simply admits that he stole two paintings, and that we caught him in the act of breaking into Mr. Jorgensen's house and trying to steal a third one. I didn't exactly say that he did it without any help, but there's nothing in it about anyone helping him. I thought that after we'd got him, Mr. Jorgensen could make him choose – either he signs the confession or we call the police. I'm betting he'll sign. Then

Mr. Jorgensen can keep the confession safe, along with the video and the still photos. And if Günther Böhm ever destroys or damages someone else's painting or work of art to use for his own so-called art, Mr. Jorgensen will turn all the material over to the police, with the recommendation that they prosecute. Jupe and Pete and I will keep an eye on him and all his future activities."

"That's a very ingenious idea," said Jupiter approvingly. "Would you be willing to keep the confession and the photographic material safe, Mr. Jorgensen?"

"Absolutely," Per Jorgensen said.

"It's a great idea, and the confession you wrote is terrific," Mallory said. "Simple and to the point. But since Böhm is always bragging about how rich he is, maybe we can also get him to contribute money to the fund that Lyle and Cornelius have started to save the Voronin murals. That would be real justice!"

"I'm not sure that will be as easy as getting him to sign the confession," Bob said, "but I really like the idea."

By now the color was fading from the sky, and Bob was beginning to feel they should get to the woodshed when Jupiter spoke up.

"The sun will presumably set again tomorrow, but only tonight will Günther Böhm be breaking and entering Mr. Jorgensen's cabin. I think we should go up."

"Yes, yes," Jorgensen said, leaping to his feet. He clipped Brigitte back onto her lead and then took off for his house, up the trail, at a brisk pace. The others scrambled after him.

Bob noticed Jupiter was a bit out of breath as they took their places in the Günther Böhm blind.

"Are you O.K., Jupe?" he asked.

Jupiter looked at him with a touch of annoyance. "I've discovered I'm not quite in the shape that you and Pete and Mallory are in," he said. "I will have to work on it."

For a while the six of them were quiet, but then Mallory said, "You know, I've been thinking about the title for Bob's next case report – at least if things work out tonight. I'm sure Bob has thought of this already, but I think it should be called *The Mystery of the Factitious Falconer* – and only partly because Leif's grandfather and Bjørn Kalberg referred to Aksel Olsen's paintings as 'counterfeit.'"

"I *had* thought of that already!" Bob said, with both surprise and pleasure.

"Factitious is a word in the English language?" Leif asked in surprise.

"None of us had ever heard it, either," Bob said. "But the moment Freya found it in her Norwegian/English dictionary, I knew I would want to use it if we ever got this case solved."

"Did you doubt that you would?" asked Per Jorgensen. "From what I've seen, The Three Investigators solve all of them! And if 'factitious' means 'counterfeit,' as you say – "

"Or fake, or phony, or bogus, or artificial – " Jupiter interjected.

"Then it could also refer to people like Günther Böhm," Per Jorgensen concluded.

"That's exactly what I was going to say!" said Mallory. "So the title would not only refer to the mystery of the Aksel Olsen paintings – and to the members of the Norwegian Resistance keeping their secret work secret! – but also to the type of people who think it would be just fine to destroy the Voronin murals."

"People who like power over other people," Bob said, nodding in agreement.

"Dangerous and ruthless opportunists," said Per Jorgensen.

And then the six of them were quiet, staring out into the gathering darkness, waiting for Günther Böhm's car to wend its way down the driveway. All around him, Bob could hear the sounds of the California night – the wind off the ocean, the occasional hoot of an owl, the swish of tires above them as cars passed on the highway.

Bob was taken aback when he suddenly saw two small circles of light in the darkness. It took him a moment to understand that Günther Böhm had parked his car somewhere on the edge of the highway, and that he and Dika were walking down the driveway holding flashlights. All six of them tensed, almost at once, and the air was electric with the power of their focus.

The moon had not yet risen, and both Böhm and Dika were wearing all black, so they were largely invisible. Bob could see them only in the reflected light of their flashlights. They were remarkably quiet, until Böhm stumbled and almost fell; the air was split as he swore in German.

"You say this place belongs to a movie star?" Böhm said. "And he cannot even pave his driveway? Ach du lieber! No matter! Soon the Munch will be mine, and I will shred it, and the world will notice, and I will be famous."

He gathered himself together and proceeded more slowly. Once or twice the erratic swing of one of the flashlight beams hit the woodshed, but the six of them were well-concealed behind a partial wall and a stack of wood. Böhm and Dika began whispering to one another as they got closer to the house. Bob watched as they paused before the door, with its panel of six windows divided by wooden strips.

At Böhm's urging, Dika took out a small leather pouch from which she removed a suction cup and a glass cutter. She affixed the suction cup to the lowest window, closest to the door lock and handle, and then carefully etched a circle in the glass big enough for her arm to go through. When she was finished, she put away the cutter, grabbed the suction cup, and popped out the glass circle. Wasting no time, she reached through the hole she'd made, unlocked the lock, and opened the door.

In the light from the flashlight, Bob caught a glimpse of Böhm's face. He looked mean and determined, almost feral. He hissed something at Dika that Bob couldn't catch. Böhm and Dika walked into Jorgensen's house and shut the door behind them.

Led by Per Jorgensen, the six of them left the woodshed and took up a position in the middle of the driveway where they could keep watch over every exit from the house.

"Pete," Jorgensen said. "You hold Brigitte. And listen carefully, the four of you. If there is any catching of Herr Böhm to be done, Leif and I will be doing it. We will be more than enough for him."

As if in response to not being needed, Mallory leaned her head toward Bob's and whispered, "Why don't the two of us go and watch the show though a window? If you're going to write about it afterwards, it would be great for you to actually see it."

"That's true," Bob whispered back.

The two of them slipped around the corner of the house. Mallory went first and Bob followed, and when they got to the deck, they climbed up and ducked under its railing, edging quickly along the exterior wall to where the panels of glass began. Mallory crouched so that Bob could stand above her, and the two of them peered around the corner to see what was going on inside Per Jorgensen's house.

It was dark in there – Jorgensen had left no lights on – but as Bob watched, the room exploded with light. In the camera's flash, Bob saw Böhm reaching for the photographic reproduction of the Aksel Olsen falconer on the wall. Böhm seemed to jump a foot in the air and started screaming. Two seconds later, the flash went off again.

In the interval, Böhm had turned to Dika with an exaggerated expression of fear and surprise on his face. Bob watched as the camera went off at two-second intervals. Each flash seemed like an electric shock that went through Günther Böhm, catching him and Dika in what looked like a herky-jerky silent movie, and a very funny one from where Bob was standing. Every gesture, every expression was pushed almost beyond belief.

Böhm was the quintessence of rage, or disbelief, or terror. His eyes bulged, his Adam's apple bobbed, his mouth hung wide open. He threw his arms in the air, splayed his fingers, stumbled and almost fell, reached for Dika and then thought better of it, turned again to the supposed painting on the wall, reached for it, yelled again in surprise, jumped in the air, and then rushed to the door he had broken in through. He had certainly lost his cool as a suave international artist looking life in the eye.

Both Mallory and Bob were laughing as they quickly retraced their steps. They were able to see Böhm and Dika, flashlights waving, rush up the driveway, only to be confronted by a wall of dark-clad figures.

"Stop!" ordered Per Jorgensen.

Dika stopped at once, but Böhm, fueled by adrenaline, kept right on coming, like a linebacker hoping to tackle the quarterback.

"Gaaaah!" he screamed. He plowed into Leif, who went down on his back, as Pete and Jupiter jumped out of the way.

As Böhm tried to scramble to his feet, Per Jorgensen tackled him, and Böhm went down like a ton of bricks. Bob had never really understood the expression before, but now he did — Böhm went down heavily, all at once, and making quite a loud noise.

But Bob was utterly amazed as Böhm somehow staggered to his feet yet once more and started running again — this time toward the ocean. The moon had come out and a dim light suffused the scene. Bob could see the beginnings of the path they had now taken twice to get down to the beach, and he could see that Böhm had seen it too. What did the man think he could do if he got down to the sea? Run along the coast? Swim to safety? He was clearly almost crazed.

"Coward!" Pete yelled at the top of his voice.

Bob and the others stared in amazement

at the unfolding events – a wild and unhinged man on a collision course with the Pacific Ocean. Per Jorgensen had remained calm in the face of everything that had happened and now he said to Pete, quite placidly, "I think you should let Brigitte off her leash."

Pete knelt down and did as he'd been told, and when Per Jorgensen said, "Go get him, girl," Bob watched, openmouthed, as Brigitte didn't hesitate but took off like a shot after Günther Böhm.

As the six of them and Dika hurried to the path to follow Böhm, they heard a screech, a thud, a series of high expressions of alarm – "Aye aye aye ayee!" – another thud and another screech. When they got to the beach, all of them a little shaky from the quick descent, they discovered, in the beam of Dika's flashlight, a curious tableau.

Böhm had tumbled head-first onto the sand and now lay on his stomach. Brigitte had grabbed his ankle and held it gingerly between her teeth. Böhm was shrieking in fear and alarm. It was clear to Bob that Brigitte had jumped up on Böhm's back and pushed him down and was now patiently awaiting more instructions from her master.

"Geh von mir runter, du räudige Sau,"

Böhm screamed.

"Brigitte!" Per Jorgensen said. "Come!" Instantly Brigitte let go of Böhm's ankle and came to sit by Jorgensen.

Groaning and swearing, Böhm got slowly to his feet. "I'll report you and your dog!" he yelled at Jorgensen.

"No, you won't," Jorgensen retorted. "By the way, she doesn't speak German. And no one calls my dog a 'mangy cur.'" He walked toward Böhm glowering, and Böhm cowered before him.

Just then, Böhm caught sight of Mallory. "I can't believe you even brought a journalist!" he yelled with what seemed to Bob to be an odd relief.

Mallory started laughing.

"What is so funny?" Böhm asked, affronted. "I am a citizen of the world, young lady! I want you to tell that world how I have been maltreated."

"Perhaps she can tell the world what a criminal you are, instead," said Jupiter. "We have video footage of you and your confederate breaking into Per Jorgensen's house, as well as thirty still photos I think quite surprised you. And by the way, the Edvard Munch painting you hoped to destroy is safe."

"It was a trap!" Böhm said.

"Indeed," Jupiter said. "A very cunning one. And one from which I do not think you are likely to escape."

"I do not want to go to jail," Günther Böhm said nervously. "And really, what I did was not so bad when you think of the truly bad things that people sometimes do."

"Yeah," Pete said. "Like wearing purple shoelaces. But don't worry. We have a better plan than that for you."

"Come on," Per Jorgensen said. "Let's go back to my house. We have a lot to discuss with this miscreant."

They decided to put Böhm right in the middle of them, so Jupiter went first, followed by Pete and Leif and Dika.

Then came Günther Böhm.

He was a mess. There was an abrasion on his forehead from where he had fallen in the sand, and his pants were ripped from the scramble down the hillside. His glasses were broken, and he kept squinting. One of his hands was bleeding. He trudged upwards, his head hung low. Behind him was Per Jorgensen, with Brigitte on a leash. Böhm did not seem to need reminding that Brigitte was following him with some eagerness.

Mallory and Bob were last up the hillside, which was fine with Bob. It was a lovely summer night. The air off the ocean was cool, and the moonlight glittered on the water, millions of silver scales. Bob felt pretty certain that Günther Böhm would sign the confession he had written and go back to Germany with his tail between his legs. In that, he would differ from Brigitte – a German Shepherd who would stay in America with her Danish master, and who was wagging her tail in celebration of a job very well done!

15

A Factitious Falconer

It was three days later, and that morning when Jupiter had woken up, it had taken him a moment to remember that it was his fourteenth birthday, and that tonight, he and Pete and Bob would be hosting a party in Isabella Chang's back garden. The delay in remembering was because the first thing he'd thought of was the fencing lesson he'd soon be having. He'd gone to bed thinking about how much he'd liked the lessons he'd had so far, and how right he'd been when he'd told Bob that being a fencer was a lot like being an investigator trying to outwit an adversary.

Fencing was, at one and the same moment, like nothing he'd ever done before and like something he'd been doing all his life. When he was fencing, he felt satisfaction at the fact that, though he was constrained by the sport's rules, he had freedom within those rules to shape his response.

Now, he was done with his lesson and was standing in the lobby of the Center for Falconry and Fencing looking at Aksel Olsen's portrait of his friend Bjørn Kalberg. It had been returned to the Center and now hung again where Jupiter had first seen it.

"The painting is just as good as I remember it," Jupiter said.

"And happily, none the worse for wear," Worthington said.

It had been a close call, Jupiter thought. The man Günther Böhm had hired to strip the paintings had begun to strip the six Böhm had managed to buy when he had realized that the initials on the gauntlets were a clue. When he'd told Günther Böhm, Böhm had ordered the stripping work to be stopped until he had his hands on the Munch – the only painting he really wanted.

At The Three Investigators' strong suggestion, Böhm had decided to return the two stolen paintings to their owners, and both Per Jorgensen and the Center for Falconry and Fencing had agreed with the judgment of the Three Investigators: they thought the painting Aksel Olsen had done was superior to the one beneath it.

"I thought Günther Böhm acted pretty well, in the end," Worthington said, turning to Jupiter. "All things considered."

"That is a matter of some contention,"

Jupiter said. "If you mean that he acted as a sane man would act, then yes. It was a welcome change from his deranged world-citizen performance."

Worthington laughed. "I must say that his signature on the confession was full of florid flourishes."

"I expect he thinks it's also a 'work of art,'" Jupiter said.

"And thanks for showing me those still photographs," said Worthington, smiling. "Whenever I need a good laugh, I'll think of them."

At this, Worthington surprised Jupiter greatly by suddenly imitating Böhm's expression in several of the photos — eyes bulging, mouth wide open in alarm, fingers splayed. Jupiter couldn't help it — he started laughing himself.

"Sometimes, Worthington," he said, "I forget that, long before you knew us, you were a professional actor."

"Yes, indeed, Master Jones," Worthington said. "Thank you for remembering."

As he and Worthington were taking one last look at the Olsen painting, Jupiter saw Mr. Hutchinson walking hurriedly across the courtyard, waving his hand. He entered the lobby with a big smile on his face.

"There you two are!" he said. "Joanna Schultz called me to say you were here, and I didn't want you to get away before I could thank you in person. I am delighted to have the painting back. And I'm so glad we were able to begin your instruction in fencing!"

"Yes," Jupiter said, shaking Mr. Hutchinson's hand. "I've very much enjoyed it. And we were very happy to help. If you ever need us in future –"

"I'll keep you well in mind," said Mr. Hutchinson.

Jupiter went to the receptionist's window to thank Joanna Schultz and to say goodbye, and then he and Worthington went out into the morning sunshine. In the Center's parking lot, as Worthington walked around the back of the Flex, he started.

"Why, the chimera sticker has been scraped off the back window!" he said.

"Yes," Jupiter said. "We're putting the new one – our logo – on later today. What better day to do that than the day of our birthday party!"

When Worthington parked the Flex back at the Salvage Yard, he clapped Jupiter on the arm.

"Happy birthday, Jupiter," he said. "I'm sure this will be an excellent year for you, and for The Three Investigators."

Jupiter smiled, a bit embarrassed.

"Now I'll be back later this afternoon to take you three to Wally and Isabella's. See you then!" Waving gaily he got into his Mini-Cooper and sped off.

Jupiter knew that Pete, Bob, and Mallory would be waiting for him in the outdoor workshop, so he lost no time.

When Pete saw Jupiter, he let out a whoop. "You're here at last!" he said. "We've been waiting for you to start our wrap-up of the case!"

"Let's take it into Headquarters," Jupiter said. They all trooped in through Easy Three, and as Mallory preceded him, Jupiter thought how few people other than he, Pete, and Bob had ever been in Headquarters. Now it seemed perfectly natural for Mallory to go in with them, and as they settled themselves around the desk, all four started talking about the fact that the signed confession, the video of the break-in, and the photographs were now in Per Jorgensen's possession.

To Jupiter's surprise, Mallory had even managed to convince Günther Böhm to donate generously to Lyle and Cornelius's fund to save the Voronin murals – though he had not done so out of the newly-reformed goodness of his heart. No, Mallory had made it very clear that, since she was not an official member of The Three Investigators, she did not feel bound by the vow he, Pete, and Bob had taken to keep Günther Böhm's illegal actions secret as long as he continued to abide by his pledge not to destroy or harm anyone else's art.

In fact, she insisted that she would immediately tell the newspapers, the police, and anyone else who would listen, if he did not donate to the fund the amount of money he had promised to pay Dika for her work in stealing the paintings. Mallory had been flinty and convincing, and finally Böhm had written a check, signing it with the same ridiculous signature. Even now he was packing up his so-called artwork and preparing to return to Berlin.

As for Dika Horváth, since Böhm never suspected that she'd cooperated with Mallory, she'd stayed out of the hands of both the police and the immigration authorities. In thanks for her decision to help catch her blackmailer, Mr. Mueller had offered to pay her what Böhm had promised, and now she, too, would soon be leaving the country and returning to Romania. And, of course, with the school year bearing down, Werner would be going back to Germany as well. It was a regular exodus!

But the paintings that Mr. Mueller had bought at auction in Germany two years before would be staying in the United States. Though the ones Günther Böhm had purchased were legally his again, and could have gone back to Germany with him, now that he couldn't destroy them, he saw no point in owning them, and sometime later in the fall they would join an auction of minor 20th century artists' paintings at an auction house in California.

As for the Munch, Matthias Mueller could not have been happier to have come into possession of such a beautiful, early painting by such an important 20th century artist, and although eventually he would be giving it to a museum, in the meanwhile, he wanted to keep it in his house, to enjoy it.

He'd insisted on thanking The Three Investigators and Mallory for the role they had played in the Munch's recovery and restoration by giving them what Jupiter thought was a very generous check. As they had done with the reward from Isabella Chang at the beginning of the summer – though this time Mallory was included – they divided the sum into five equal parts. Each of them had money to add to their college funds, and the fifth part went into The Three Investigators' bank account.

While Jupiter was considering how to start the discussion about all these events, Bob was booting up the firm's desktop computer to the newly redesigned website for The Jones Salvage Yard, which had finally gone live, after a long summer in the planning.

"Look at that!" said Bob. "The web designer did a terrific job. And look at the photos Mallory took of the things the Salvage Yard has for sale! And her descriptions are brilliant!"

Jupiter was pleased at how professional it all looked. He could see that the photos and Mallory's descriptions were likely to generate a lot of interest and a lot of sales.

"It's very impressive," Jupiter said.

"It just went live about an hour ago," Bob said.

"How's Aunt Mathilda taking it?" Jupiter asked.

"From what we can tell," Pete said, "she's fanning herself and having a lie-down. She's pretty excited."

"The Three Investigators have certainly

seen a lot of changes this summer," Mallory said. "You've got a new logo. And new business cards, and a new Salvage Yard website, and Bob's reports. Now all you need is a new Headquarters!"

Jupiter wondered, for a moment, whether this required a reply and then decided to let it go.

"I'm so glad we got to see Cornelius rub the last bit of Aksel Olsen's painting from the lost Edvard Munch," Bob said. "Those colors really seemed to glow! It was almost as if the painting were alive."

"I can't believe we really rescued a lost masterpiece!" Pete said.

"And 'we' is the right word," Jupiter said. "It was a true team effort. Pete, you had the great idea of contacting Per Jorgensen in the first place, and he proved to be invaluable. Bob, you were the first to figure out that the Olsen paintings must have been painted over other paintings. And Mallory, the whole plan for trapping Günther Böhm was yours."

"So what did *you* do, Jupe?" Pete asked.

"He thought a lot," Bob said, and everyone laughed.

But then Mallory surprised Jupiter by saying, "He did what he always seems to do.

He used his head, listened to his instincts, and kept his eye on the big picture. And, of course, he figured out that the marks in the grass at the Center had been made by a mini-trampoline, and that the initials in the falconer paintings were a code!"

Though Jupiter didn't know exactly what to say to this, he shook his head ruefully. "I should have figured the code out sooner," he said.

"No, you shouldn't," Pete said. "I was joking just now, but you've always been an excellent leader. Way back in kindergarten, you were already decisive. And even though the three of us are very different, you saw from the start that we would be far more effective together than any of us could ever be alone."

Once again, Jupiter was a bit embarrassed, but he smiled his thanks. "We've come a long way together, Second. And this case was quite satisfactory, in the end."

"It's too bad we couldn't keep the Munch as a memento," Bob said. Jupiter saw he was only half kidding.

"I like what we got!" Pete said, pointing to the crowded wall of Headquarters where a falconer's glove and gauntlet had been pinned. After Günther Böhm had signed the confession as well as the check for the fund to protect the Voronin murals, he'd stalked out of Per Jorgensen's house, taking Dika with him. They'd watched the lonely stabs of two flashlight beams as they moved up the driveway to the highway, and then the boys and Mallory and Leif had gotten ready to leave.

"Before you go," Per Jorgensen had said, "I have something for you."

He'd gone into the living room and returned with one of the gauntlets they had seen the first time they'd been there.

"I bought this after *The Seventh Messenger* wrapped," he said, "when I planned to find time in my schedule to also be a falconer. No such luck. I thought you might want it. As a memento of the time we worked together to send our factitious falconer on his way."

Though there were no elaborate designs on the gauntlet, as there were on the one Jorgensen had worn in the movie, Jupiter thought he liked it even better. He let his eyes run over the other mementoes from the summer's cases – the gold assayer's scale, the set of two conflicting history books, the California recruiting poster, the dagger with the damascene blade, the carving of the humpback whale. And next to them the glove and gauntlet.

It had been a rewarding summer, he thought – full of surprises and rewards and successes. The Three Investigators had solved six fascinating and difficult cases, each very different from the others; they'd met a lot of people they truly liked and admired; he'd discovered a whole missing branch of his family and learned that he was the son of two astronomers – who had named him after a planet; he'd started fencing; and he was slowly getting to know Mallory MacLeod, who turned out to be a rare find. Just as Jupiter thought this, Mallory spoke.

"You're almost out of wall space," she remarked – a simple matter of fact. "If you're as busy next summer, you'll be completely out."

Mallory was right, Jupiter noted. Next summer, he might have to give some serious thought to the idea of a new Headquarters. He glanced at his watch and was surprised at how quickly time had flown. "If we're going to put the new logo on the back window of the Flex and still have time to get ready for the party," he said, standing up, "we'd better go now."

Before he left, he picked up a wooden ruler and a black marking pencil from the desk.

They barreled out of Headquarters,

closed Easy Three behind them, and clustered around the Flex, which Worthington had parked near the office. Connor O'Malley, who had designed the logo in keeping with Pete's great idea, had had various sizes made. Pete had left a large decal in the box it had come in, and everyone watched as he opened the box and took the decal out.

"Before you take off the backing, let me mark exactly where it's going," Jupiter said. He carefully measured both the decal and the window, then put tiny black marks around the space where the decal would go.

Pete turned the decal over and held it steady while Jupiter removed the backing.

"Careful, careful," Pete said. "We don't want to mess this up and have to start over!" He and Jupiter each took an edge and, holding their breaths, they maneuvered until they were holding it right above the rear window, then carefully placed the top of the decal on the markings Jupiter had made and let gravity pull the rest of it into place. It went on without a ripple or a bulge, it was both square and trim, and boy! did it look great!

There was the golden eagle − with which, Jupiter had to admit, he felt a certain kinship. It had a wide wingspan, and its excellent vision allowed it to see what others missed. The main body of the chimera was the bobcat – Bob – an animal known for its stealth and patience. Like Bob it was solid, dependable – The Three Investigators' center. And although the big-horned sheep was only there in parts, those parts were fierce, fearless, and wild – an avatar of the warrior spirit. Pete.

"This was a great idea, Pete," Mallory said, and Pete looked very pleased.

"I couldn't agree more," Jupiter said. "A new logo for a new Three Investigators! Now everyone go home, and get changed, and get ready! Mallory, your mother's taking you, right?" Mallory nodded. "Bob and Pete, let's meet back here at six, and Worthington will drive us over. I'll call the caterer one last time and make sure she's delivering all the food we've ordered, as well as the paper plates and napkins and cups."

And at just a little after six, there the four of them were – Worthington driving, with Pete riding shotgun, and Jupiter and Bob in back. Almost eleven weeks had passed since they'd first met Isabella Chang at Hector Sebastian's house for their first case of the summer, and maybe nine weeks since they'd first ridden their bikes to her house for dinner, after she'd received the money from the gold nuggets they'd discovered in Auburn. It seemed like longer, Jupiter thought.

The front door of Isabella's house was wide open and Wally and Isabella came out to greet them.

"Come in, come in," Wally said. "Although none of the guests are here yet – well, none except for Charlotte Mitchell – they will be soon!"

"Hector Sebastian called to wish you all a very happy birthday," Isabella said. "The caterer came about an hour ago. What extravagance! There's enough for an army."

"Good!" said Pete. "I feel like a whole platoon!"

Isabella's backyard had never looked so festive, Jupiter thought. The grass had been freshly trimmed and was vibrantly green from the hidden sprinklers. On the patio, by the koi pond, were two folding tables where the food had been laid out. Next to it were galvanized tubs of ice filled to overflowing with drinks, and a grill which would be lit later on. What a birthday party! Jupiter thought. The caterers had delivered everything they were supposed to, and Charlotte Mitchell – who they'd first met right here at Isabella's house –

seemed to be making sure that everything was set out properly.

As usual, she was dressed in bright, eccentric clothing – this time it was pantaloons and a tie-dyed shirt with a purple scarf around her neck. She turned to wave to them as Pete said, "I can hardly wait to introduce her to Connor O'Malley. I just know they're going to like each other!"

Jupiter felt a little awkward when Pete repeated this to Charlotte as soon as she came up to them, but Charlotte seemed interested in Pete's remark, and when Connor proved to be the first guest to arrive, and Pete introduced him to Charlotte, Jupiter had to admit that they *did* seem to like each other right away.

In fact, they got along like a house afire.

Soon other people were arriving – with Rafael Solares and his partner Elena down from Isla Vista for the day, and Wally seeming pleased that they were there. That wasn't surprising, Jupiter reflected. After all, Wally had known Rafael for years and years; he was like a second son to Wally – or maybe a first son, now that Wally's real son, Russell, had been discovered to be a criminal.

As more and more people arrived – Bob's and Pete's parents, Mallory and her mother, Aunt Mathilda and Uncle Titus, Leif and Magnus and Freya Haldorsson, Lyle and Cornelius, Matthias Mueller and Werner and Dika, and also Mallory's friend Califia Garcia-Williams and the historian Phillipa Paxton who The Three Investigators had met in their second case of the summer – Jupiter kept looking for, but not seeing, the Pelletier family. *His* family, really. Jupiter had discovered the Pelletiers up in Jackson earlier that summer, but though he'd written e-mails to his two young second cousins, and had called his great-aunt two or three times, he hadn't seen any of them since he'd first met them over the 4th of July weekend.

As he was standing talking with Pete, Bob, and Mallory and drinking a soda he had taken from one of the galvanized tubs, Bob's cellphone rang; it was John Pelletier saying that he and his family would be about an hour late. There had been a construction delay on I-5. Bob reassured them they'd be in time for dinner.

Just then, Freya, Leif, and Magnus came up to get drinks of their own, and soon Bob had been corralled away and was sitting talking with the Haldorssons – and from what Jupiter could see, especially with Freya. Other guests had sorted themselves into what also seemed natural groups: Bob and Pete's parents were talking with Uncle Titus, Aunt Mathilda, and Mallory's mother; Wally and Isabella were sitting with Rafael and Elena; and Charlotte Mitchell and Connor O'Malley had been joined by Worthington and Phillipa Paxton.

As for Matthias Mueller, Werner, and Dika, they had gravitated toward Lyle and Cornelius, while Pete was sitting and talking with Califia Garcia-Williams – who, Jupiter suspected, Pete had a crush on.

As Jupiter looked around the backyard, it was like having an entire, satisfying summer come to life. It felt good to be by himself for a moment, and he'd taken a seat under one of the trees at the back of the yard when he saw Mallory walking toward him.

The last time they'd been alone together had been when they'd broken into the warehouse near Santa Barbara, and later, when they'd been in the bow of Rafael Solares's boat, the *Rainbow Bridge*. He was glad to see her away from the others now.

"Hi, Jupiter," she said. "Do you mind if I sit with you for a while? I was talking to Califia about that horrible New Resistance Co-Op before Pete came along. I still can't believe

312

those people had the gall to give themselves a name like that."

Jupiter nodded. "Aksel Olsen and Bjørn Kalberg and Håkon Haldorsson are the kind of people it's good to be able to admire. They were smart and tenacious and ingenious, as well as courageous. And they knew that it was as important to protect other people's accomplishments as it was to protect their own."

"That actually sounds a lot like The Three Investigators," Mallory said. She was looking away, but Jupiter could tell she was smiling.

She paused and took a deep breath. "You probably already know this, but I've had so much fun hanging out with you this summer. I'm almost sorry school's about to start. I love studying, but I'm going to miss using my mind the way I have on some of The Three Investigators' cases. And by next summer who knows what you'll be doing – or me either."

For a moment, Jupiter felt as if he had heard this before somewhere – as if the moment was one he'd already lived. Then he realized he was simply having what the French called a *déjà vu*. The scientific explanation for such moments was that they had been stored in your memory before they reached your conscious mind.

Whether or not that was what had just happened, the fact was that Jupiter had gotten used to Mallory helping with their investigations. In fact, as the summer had gone on, he'd come to depend on her more and more. She was resourceful, she needed little direction, and she got along well with all of them. The idea of proceeding without her in future seemed unsatisfactory. But what was he to say? A firm called The Three Investigators couldn't have a fourth member.

Then he thought of their card – on which he and Pete were listed as the First and Second Investigators, but Bob was listed as Records and Research. He also remembered what Pete had said about him being a natural leader. It might have embarrassed Jupiter when he'd said it, but it had been true enough, he thought.

Although Pete and Bob were as different from one another as a bobcat was from a big-horned sheep – and both of them different from Jupiter – he'd had a sense that their strengths could be pooled. That was an important part of what a leader was – someone who knew how to get very different people to work together. Also, someone who knew how to use people's talents and knowledge to the greatest possible advantage.

So Jupiter said, "When we were in Headquarters before, I suggested that solving our cases has always been a true team effort – and you've been an important part of that effort lately."

Jupiter paused. "I hope you'll work with us again next summer. I know that Bob and Pete would like it, and I'd like it, too. Maybe we could give you the title of Special Consultant to The Three Investigators. You'd be the only Special Consultant we've ever had."

Mallory just had time to look startled, then delighted, when her mother started walking toward them, talking to someone on her cellphone. Mallory nodded once at Jupiter. "I'd love that!" she said. Then she leapt to her feet to intercept her mother before she reached the tree under which she and Jupiter had been sitting.

Jupiter, though, remained sitting – happy with what he'd just done, looking at the people assembled for the party, and thinking about the case The Three Investigators had just wrapped up. It had forced him to think about art, and artists, and honesty, in a whole new way. Life itself was a kind of art form, really. A fencing match with the cosmos – in which you might be constrained by the nature of the world around you, but in which you always had the freedom to shape your response to what you couldn't change.

And in a time when too many people were defining who they were by who they *weren't* – when, as Matthias Mueller had pointed out, a lot of human beings seemed to look for other human beings to hate, or disapprove of – Jupiter felt a sense of satisfaction that that wasn't what The Three Investigators were all about. While he wouldn't want to call himself and Bob and Pete falconers, exactly, he thought it might be permissible to call all of them fencers, of a sort. A band of brothers who understood the difference between an enemy and an adversary – and who could hardly wait for next summer to roll around.

Although Jupiter had no idea what cases would await them then, whatever they were, he and Pete and Bob – and now Mallory – would be ready for action. *En garde!* Jupiter thought.

ABOUT THE AUTHORS

Elizabeth Arthur

Elizabeth was born on November 15, 1953 in New York City. She is the daughter of Robert Arthur, the creator of The Three Investigators series. She was educated at Concord Academy in Concord, Massachusetts, the University of Michigan in Ann Arbor, Michigan, Notre Dame University of Nelson, British Columbia, and the University of Victoria in Victoria, British Columbia.

Before she started working on the New Three Investigators series in December of 2018, Elizabeth spent most of her life writing for adults. *Island Sojourn* – a memoir about building a house on a wilderness island in northern Canada – was published in 1980 by Harper and Row. A second memoir, *Looking For The Klondike Stone*, was published by Knopf in 1992. She is also the author of the novels *Beyond the Mountain, Bad Guys, Binding Spell, Antarctic Navigation,* and *Bring Deeps*.

Elizabeth's writing has received fellowships, grants, and awards from the Bread Loaf Writer's Conference, the Ossabaw Island Project, the Vermont Council on the Arts, and the

Indiana Arts Commission. She twice received fellowships from the National Endowment for the Arts and was the first novelist ever given an Antarctic Artists and Writers Operational Support Grant from the National Science Foundation.

Her novel *Antarctic Navigation* was chosen by the New York *Times* as a Notable Book, received a Critics' Choice Award from the San Francisco *Review of Books*, and was chosen as a Best Book of 1995 by *A Common Reader*. In 1996 the novel received the Ohioana Book Award for Fiction from the Ohioana Library Association.

Elizabeth has also taught creative writing at Miami University in Oxford, Ohio; the University of Cincinnati; and Indiana University/Purdue University of Indianapolis, where she directed the creative writing program. She and Steven Bauer met in 1980 at the Bread Loaf Writer's Conference and have been married since June of 1982.

Steven Bauer

Steven was born on September 10, 1948 in Newark, New Jersey. He was educated at Hanover Park High School in East Hanover, New Jersey, Trinity College in Hartford, Connecticut, and the University of Massachusetts in Amherst, Massachusetts. In 1970 he received a B.A. with Honors in English from Trinity, and in 1975 he received an M.F.A. in English from the University of Massachusetts.

Steven is the author of three books for young people – *Satyrday*, 1980; *The Strange and Wonderful Tale of Robert McDoodle*, 1999; and *A Cat of a Different Color*, 2000. His book of poems *Daylight Savings* was published by Gibbs Smith in 1989 and won the Peregrine Smith Poetry Prize.

Steven's work has received fellowships from the Bread Loaf Writer's Conference and the Fine Arts Work Center in Provincetown, Massachusetts. In addition, he has been given grants and awards from the American Library Association, the Parents' Choice Foundation, the Ossabaw Island Project, the Massachusetts Arts Council, and the Indiana Arts Commission.

From 1979 to 1982, Steven taught literature and creative writing at Colby College in Waterville, Maine. From 1982 to 2009 he taught at Miami University in Oxford, Ohio where he directed the graduate and under-graduate creative writing programs. In 2010 he established Hollow Tree Literary Services, an independent editing business.